Robert Rose's Favorite
CHICKEN

Robert
ROSE

ROBERT ROSE'S FAVORITE CHICKEN

Copyright © 1998 Robert Rose Inc.

Canadian Cataloguing in Publication Data

Main entry under title:

Robert Rose's favorite chicken

Includes index.

ISBN 1-896503-53-5

1. Cookery (Poultry).   I. Title: Chicken.

TX750.5.C45R62 1998   641.6'65   C98-930498-1

DESIGN AND PAGE COMPOSITION: MATTHEWS COMMUNICATIONS DESIGN
PHOTOGRAPHY: MARK T. SHAPIRO

Cover photo: (CHICKEN-VEGETABLE COBBLER, PAGE 59)

Distributed in the U.S. by:
Firefly Books (U.S.) Inc.
P.O. Box 1338
Ellicott Station
Buffalo, NY   14205

Distributed in Canada by:
Stoddart Publishing Co. Ltd.
34 Lesmill Road
North York, Ontario
M3B 2T6

ORDER LINES
Tel: (416) 499-8412
Fax: (416) 499-8313

ORDER LINES
Tel: (416) 445-3333
Fax: (416) 445-5967

Published by: Robert Rose Inc. • 156 Duncan Mill Road, Suite 12
Toronto, Ontario, Canada M3B 2N2   Tel: (416) 449-3535

Printed in Canada   234567 BP 01 00 99 98

About this book

At Robert Rose, we're committed to finding imaginative and exciting ways to provide our readers with cookbooks that offer great recipes — and exceptional value. That's the thinking behind our "Robert Rose's Favorite" series.

Here we've selected over 50 favorite chicken recipes from a number of our bestselling full-sized cookbooks: Byron Ayanoglu's *Simply Mediterranean Cooking*; Johanna Burkhard's *Comfort Food Cookbook*; Andrew Chase's *Asian Bistro Cookbook*; *New World Noodles* and *New World Chinese Cooking*, by Bill Jones and Stephen Wong; and Rose Reisman's *Light Cooking, Light Pasta* and *Enlightened Home Cooking*. As well, we've included recipes from our own *Robert Rose's Classic Pasta*.

We believe that it all adds up to great value for anyone who loves chicken.

Want to find out more about the sources of our recipes? See pages 94 and 95 for details.

Contents

Main Dishes

Pasta

Appetizers

Thai Grilled Chicken Wings

Serves 4 to 6

The fragrant marinade and glaze exemplifies the traditional Thai blend of spicy, sweet, savory and sour in one dish. Marinated wings are grilled and glazed with a Thai honey-garlic sauce. They should be threaded, Thai style, on long bamboo skewers for an exotic presentation and for grilling ease.

•

The chilies are sprinkled on at the last minute, so the heat of the dish can be adjusted to taste. The fresh uncooked chilies contrast well with the sweet-and-sour garlic glaze.

FROM
THE ASIAN BISTRO COOKBOOK BY ANDREW CHASE

3 lbs	chicken wings, about 18 pieces	1.5 kg
1 tbsp	red curry paste	15 mL
2 tbsp	fish sauce *or* 3 pounded anchovies and 1 tbsp (15 mL) soya sauce	25 mL
3 tbsp	lime juice	45 mL
1 tsp	sugar	5 mL
1 tbsp	finely chopped coriander, leaves and stems	15 mL
2 tsp	minced ginger	10 mL
1 tsp	finely chopped, deveined lime leaf (optional)	5 mL
1 tbsp	oil	15 mL
1/4 cup	honey	50 mL
1 tbsp	minced garlic	15 mL
1 to 2 tsp	finely chopped chilies, preferably bird-eye chilies	5 to 10 mL
18	long bamboo skewers, soaked in water	18
	Lime wedges for garnish	

1. Marinate wings for at least 2 hours in a mixture of curry paste, 1 tbsp (15 mL) fish sauce, 1 tbsp (15 mL) lime juice, sugar, coriander, ginger, lime leaf (if available), and oil.

2. In a small saucepan over very low heat, stir in the honey, 1 tbsp (15 mL) fish sauce, remaining 2 tbsp (25 mL) lime juice and garlic until it reaches a simmer and is well mixed; set aside.

3. Thread each wing onto a skewer, starting at the tip of the drumette through the 3 sections so the wing tip is at the tip of the skewer and the wing is stretched straight. Grill over hot charcoal or under a broiler until cooked through and nicely browned; brush with the garlic glaze, turning each wing 2 or 3 times and glazing each time. On the last turn, sprinkle with the chopped chilies to taste (they should stick to the glaze). Serve garnished with lime wedges.

Yummy Parmesan Chicken Fingers

Serves 4

TIP

Buy boneless chicken breasts when they're featured as a supermarket special and make batches of chicken fingers to freeze ahead. Use fresh (not defrosted) chicken breasts; prepare recipe as directed, placing unbaked strips on a rack set on baking sheet. Freeze until firm; transfer to a storage container. Can be frozen for up to 2 months. No need to defrost before baking.

•

You can also make extra batches of the crumb mixture and store in the freezer.

•

Instead of boneless chicken breasts, prepare skinless chicken drumsticks in the same way but bake in a 375° F (190° C) oven for 35 to 40 minutes or until tender. The butter baste gives a nice flavor, but is optional if counting calories.

FROM
THE COMFORT FOOD COOKBOOK BY JOHANNA BURKHARD

What a relief to know when you come home frazzled from a day at work, you can count on these tasty chicken fingers stashed away in your freezer. Round out the meal with rice and a steamed vegetable (like broccoli) for a dinner that's on the table in 30 minutes.

PREHEAT OVEN TO 400° F (200° C)
BAKING SHEET

1/2 cup	finely crushed soda cracker crumbs (about 16 crackers)	125 mL
1/3 cup	freshly grated Parmesan cheese	75 mL
1/2 tsp	dried basil	2 mL
1/2 tsp	dried marjoram	2 mL
1/2 tsp	paprika	2 mL
1/2 tsp	salt	2 mL
1/4 tsp	black pepper	1 mL
4	skinless boneless chicken breasts	4
1/3 cup	sour cream *or* plain yogurt (or 1 large egg, beaten)	75 mL
1	clove garlic, minced	1
2 tbsp	melted butter (optional)	25 mL

1. In a food processor combine cracker crumbs, Parmesan cheese, basil, marjoram, paprika, salt and pepper. Process to make fine crumbs. Place in shallow bowl.

2. Cut chicken breasts into 4 strips each. Place in a bowl; stir in sour cream and garlic. Using a fork, dip chicken strips in crumb mixture until evenly coated. Arrange on greased rack set on baking sheet. Brush tops lightly with melted butter, if desired.

3. Bake in preheated oven for 15 minutes or until no longer pink in center. (If frozen, bake for up to 25 minutes.)

Chicken Tortillas

TIP

Boneless turkey breast, pork or veal scallopini can replace chicken.

•

The cheese adds a creamy texture to the tortillas. Mozzarella can also be used.

MAKE AHEAD

Prepare filling early in the day and gently reheat before stuffing tortillas. Add extra stock if sauce is too thick.

FROM
ROSE REISMAN'S
ENLIGHTENED
HOME COOKING

PREHEAT OVEN TO 375° F (190° C)
BAKING SHEET SPRAYED WITH VEGETABLE SPRAY

6 oz	skinless boneless chicken breast, diced	150 g
1 tsp	vegetable oil	5 mL
1 tsp	crushed garlic	5 mL
1 cup	chopped onions	250 mL
1/2 cup	finely chopped carrots	125 mL
1 cup	tomato pasta sauce	250 mL
1 cup	canned red kidney beans, drained	250 mL
1/2 cup	chicken stock	125 mL
1 tsp	chili powder	5 mL
8	small 6-inch (15-cm) flour tortillas	8
1/2 cup	shredded Cheddar cheese (optional)	125 mL

1. In a nonstick skillet sprayed with vegetable spray, cook chicken over high heat for 2 minutes, or until done at center. Remove from skillet and set aside.

2. Reduce heat to medium and add oil to pan. Respray with vegetable spray and cook garlic, onions, and carrots for 10 minutes, or until browned and softened, stirring often. Add some water if vegetables start to burn. Add tomato sauce, beans, stock and chili powder and cook for 10 to 12 minutes or until carrots are tender, mixture has thickened and most of the liquid is absorbed. Stir in chicken and remove from heat.

3. Put 1/3 cup (75 mL) of mixture on each tortilla, sprinkle with cheese (if using) and roll up. Put on prepared baking sheet and bake for 10 minutes or until heated through.

Chicken Satay with Peanut Sauce

Serves 5

TIP

These satays can be barbecued for approximately 10 minutes or until chicken is cooked.

•

Chicken can be replaced with fresh salmon, pork or beef.

•

This sauce can be used as a marinade for beef or fish.

•

These appetizers have a fair amount of protein. Have a main course with less protein.

MAKE AHEAD

Prepare sauce up to 2 days in advance. Keep refrigerated.

FROM
ROSE REISMAN'S
ENLIGHTENED
HOME COOKING

PREHEAT OVEN TO 425°F (220°C)
BAKING PAN SPRAYED WITH VEGETABLE SPRAY

1 lb	skinless, boneless chicken breasts	500 g

Peanut Sauce

2 tbsp	peanut butter	25 mL
2 tbsp	chicken stock	25 mL
2 tbsp	chopped fresh coriander	25 mL
1 tbsp	rice wine vinegar	15 mL
1 tbsp	honey	15 mL
2 tsp	sesame oil	10 mL
2 tsp	soya sauce	10 mL
1 tsp	minced garlic	5 mL
1 tsp	minced ginger root	5 mL
1 tsp	sesame seeds, toasted	5 mL

1. In small bowl or food processor, combine peanut butter, chicken stock, coriander, vinegar, honey, sesame oil, soya sauce, garlic, ginger and sesame seeds. Set 3 tbsp (45 mL) aside.

2. Cut chicken into 1-inch (2.5 cm) cubes. Thread onto 10 small bamboo or barbecue skewers. Place skewers in prepared pan. Brush with half of the peanut sauce that has been set aside. Bake approximately 5 minutes. Turn over and brush the remaining 1 1/2 tbsp (20 mL) sauce and bake 5 more minutes or just until chicken is done. Serve with remaining peanut sauce.

Honey-Garlic Chicken Wings

Serves 8

as an appetizer or 4 as a main course

These spicy wings are always a party hit. They're deliciously messy, so be sure to have plenty of napkins on hand.

TIP

You can also partially cook the wings in the oven for the first 20 minutes and complete the cooking on the barbecue over medium heat.

•

Taste the marinade sauce before adding to the chicken wings; it should have a nice zip to it.

FROM
THE COMFORT FOOD COOKBOOK BY JOHANNA BURKHARD

PREHEAT OVEN TO 400° F (200° C)
RIMMED BAKING SHEET, LINED WITH FOIL THEN BRUSHED WITH OIL

3 lbs	chicken wings, separated and tips removed	1.5 kg
1/3 cup	soya sauce	75 mL
1/4 cup	honey	50 mL
2 tbsp	hoisin sauce	25 mL
2 tbsp	rice vinegar	25 mL
2	large cloves garlic, minced	2
2 tsp	hot pepper sauce, or more to taste	10 mL

1. Place chicken wings in a large heavy plastic bag and set in a large bowl. In a small bowl, combine soya sauce, honey, hoisin sauce, vinegar, garlic and hot pepper sauce. Pour over wings, close tightly and seal. Let marinate in fridge for several hours or overnight.

2. On prepared baking sheet, arrange wings in a single layer; bake in preheated oven for 20 minutes. Pour off pan juices and turn wings over.

3. Meanwhile, place marinade in a small saucepan. Bring to a boil over medium heat; cook 3 to 5 minutes or until slightly thickened. Baste wings liberally with marinade.

4. Bake 15 to 20 minutes more or until wings are tender and nicely glazed.

Oriental Chicken Wrapped Mushrooms

Serves 4 to 6

or makes 18 hors d'oeuvres

TIP

Tender beef is delicious with this sweet oriental sauce.

MAKE AHEAD

Refrigerate chicken in marinade early in day. Wrap chicken around mushroom caps and broil just before serving.

FROM
ROSE REISMAN BRINGS HOME LIGHT COOKING

PREHEAT BROILER
BAKING SHEET SPRAYED WITH VEGETABLE SPRAY

1 tbsp	rice wine vinegar	15 mL
1 tbsp	vegetable oil	15 mL
2 tbsp	soya sauce	25 mL
1 tsp	crushed garlic	5 mL
2 tbsp	finely chopped onion	25 mL
1 tsp	sesame oil	5 mL
2 tbsp	water	25 mL
2 tbsp	brown sugar	25 mL
1/2 tsp	sesame seeds (optional)	2 mL
12 oz	boneless skinless chicken breast	375 g
18	medium mushroom caps (without stems)	18

1. In a bowl combine vinegar, oil, soya sauce, garlic, onion, sesame oil, water, sugar, and sesame seeds (if using); mix well.

2. Cut chicken into strips about 3 inches (8 cm) long and 1 inch (2.5 cm) wide to make 18 strips. Add to bowl and marinate for 20 minutes, stirring occasionally.

3. Wrap each chicken strip around mushroom; secure with toothpick. Place on baking sheet. Broil for approximately 5 minutes or until chicken is no longer pink inside. Serve immediately.

Soups

Chicken Noodle Soup

Serves 8

Often called "Jewish penicillin," chicken soup is the perfect antidote to an oncoming cold. But there's more to its restorative powers. Rich and delicious, it can banish the winter blues and make you feel just plain good any day of the year.

TIP

You don't have to slave over the stove to make this soul-satisfying soup. Adding the chicken and the vegetables to the pot at the same time streamlines the process and does away with the chore of making stock first. The results are every bit as pleasing.

FROM
THE COMFORT FOOD COOKBOOK BY JOHANNA BURKHARD

3 lb	whole chicken *or* chicken pieces, such as legs and breasts	1.5 kg
10 cups	water (approximate)	2.5 L
1	large onion, finely chopped	1
3	carrots, peeled and chopped	3
2	stalks celery, including leaves, chopped	2
2 tbsp	chopped fresh parsley	25 mL
1/2 tsp	dried thyme	2 mL
2 tsp	salt	10 mL
1/4 tsp	pepper	1 mL
1	bay leaf	1
2 cups	medium or broad egg noodles	500 mL
1 cup	finely diced zucchini *or* small cauliflower florets	250 mL
2 tbsp	chopped fresh dill *or* parsley	25 mL

1. Rinse chicken; remove as much skin and excess fat as possible. Place in a large stockpot; add water to cover. Bring to a boil over high heat; using a slotted spoon, skim off foam as it rises to the surface.

2. Add onion, carrots, celery, parsley, thyme, salt, pepper and bay leaf. Reduce heat to medium–low; cover and simmer for about 1 1/4 hours or until chicken is tender.

3. Remove chicken with slotted spoon and place in a large bowl; let cool slightly. Pull chicken meat off the bones, discarding skin and bones. Cut meat into bite-sized pieces. Reserve 2 cups (500 mL) for soup. (Use remainder for casseroles and sandwiches.)

4. Skim fat from surface of soup; bring to a boil. Add cubed chicken, noodles, zucchini and dill; cook for 10 minutes or until noodles and vegetables are tender. Remove bay leaf. Adjust seasoning with salt and pepper to taste.

Aromatic Chicken Stock

About 18 cups

(4.5 L)

Basic chicken stock is probably the best liquid to add to any sauce — whether meat-, fish- or vegetable-based.

•

Chicken necks and backs are usually available at the meat counter of grocery stores.

•

The stock will keep refrigerated for about 1 week or it can be frozen and kept for up to 2 months.

FROM

NEW WORLD NOODLES BY BILL JONES & STEPHEN WONG

5 lb	chicken backs and necks, rinsed to remove any blood	2 kg
3	large onions, peeled and roughly chopped	3
3	carrots, peeled and roughly chopped	3
3	celery stalks, roughly chopped	3
1/2	garlic head	1/2
1	piece ginger root, about 2 inches (5 cm) long	1
1	small handful mixed herbs (cilantro, basil, etc.)	1
5	whole black peppercorns	5
1 tbsp	salt (preferably sea salt)	15 mL
20 cups	water	5 L

1. Place ingredients in a large stockpot, adding more water, if necessary, to cover. Bring mixture to a boil; reduce heat and simmer gently for 3 hours, skimming occasionally to remove any foam or impurities that rise to the top. Try not to let the mixture boil or the broth will be cloudy.

2. Strain into a container and cool to room temperature before refrigerating. (If hot stock is placed directly in the fridge, it will sometimes sour.) For a more intensely flavored stock, let liquid cool and remove any fat from the top; return stock to pot and, over low heat, simmer until volume is reduced by half.

Chicken and Tomato Soup with Glass Noodle Egg Drop Dumplings

Serves 4

as a main course or 6 as a starter

FROM
NEW WORLD NOODLES BY
BILL JONES & STEPHEN WONG

Marinade

2 tsp	minced ginger root	10 mL
1 tbsp	dry sherry *or* white wine	15 mL
1/4 tsp	salt	1 mL
1 tbsp	soya sauce	15 mL
2 tsp	cornstarch	10 mL
8 oz	boneless chicken breast, cut into thin strips 2 inches (5 cm) long	250 g
2 oz	bean thread noodles *or* angel hair pasta	50 g
2	large eggs, beaten	2

Broth

6 cups	chicken stock	1.5 L
3	large tomatoes, peeled, seeded and coarsely chopped	3
1	small onion, sliced	1
1/2	English cucumber, cut into 2-inch (5 cm) long matchsticks *or* 1 cup (250 mL) fresh or frozen peas	1/2
	Salt and white pepper, to taste	
2 tbsp	coarsely chopped cilantro leaves	25 mL

1. In a bowl combine ingredients for marinade. Add chicken and set aside for 20 minutes.

2. In a heatproof bowl or pot, cover noodles with boiling water and soak for 3 minutes. (If using pasta, prepare according to package directions.) Drain and chop into 1/2-inch (1 cm) lengths.

3. In a medium-sized bowl, whisk eggs. Add noodle pieces, mix well and set aside.

4. In a large pot, combine chicken stock, tomatoes and onion; bring to a boil. Reduce heat to low, cover and simmer for 15 minutes. Add chicken and return to a boil. Simmer for 2 minutes or until chicken is cooked. Bring mixture back to a rolling boil and slowly pour noodle mixture into the soup, stirring vigorously. Add cucumber and cook for 1 minute to warm through. Season with salt and white pepper, garnish with chopped cilantro and serve immediately.

Chili, Chicken, Bean and Pasta Stew

2 tsp	vegetable oil	10 mL
2 tsp	crushed garlic	10 mL
1 cup	chopped onions	250 mL
8 oz	ground chicken	250 g
1	can (19 oz [540 mL]) crushed tomatoes	1
2 1/2 cups	chicken stock	625 mL
1 1/2 cups	diced peeled potatoes	375 mL
1/2 cup	canned red kidney beans, drained	125 mL
1/2 cup	canned chickpeas, drained	125 mL
2 tbsp	tomato paste	25 mL
1 tbsp	chili powder	15 mL
2 tsp	dried basil	10 mL
1 tsp	dried oregano	5 mL
Pinch	cayenne	Pinch
1/3 cup	macaroni	75 mL

1. In a large nonstick saucepan, heat oil; sauté garlic and onions until softened, approximately 5 minutes.

2. Add chicken and cook, stirring to break up chunks, until no longer pink; pour off any fat.

3. Add tomatoes, stock, potatoes, kidney beans, chickpeas, tomato paste, chili powder, basil, oregano and cayenne. Cover and reduce heat; simmer for 40 minutes, stirring occasionally.

4. Add pasta; cook until firm to the bite, approximately 10 minutes.

Lemon-Scented Chicken Soup with Green Tomato

Serves 4

In the Philippines, cooking a chicken typically involves cutting up the whole bird (including head and feet), searing the pieces with fragrant seasonings and then simmering them in water with a variety of vegetables — such as taro root, chayote and/or green papaya — often flavored with the juice of sour green tamarind or sour citrus juice. Here I have adapted this style to create a soup suitable for serving as a first course. Since we don't use a whole chicken, we must boost the taste with chicken broth. The chicken meat is quickly sautéed with seasonings and poached in the broth with green tomato and finished with lemon. The result is a really full-flavored and unusual soup.

FROM
THE ASIAN BISTRO
COOKBOOK BY ANDREW
CHASE

3	strips lemon peel, about the size of your little finger	3
1 tsp	cornstarch	5 mL
1/4 tsp	black pepper	1 mL
12 oz	skinless boneless chicken breasts or thighs, cut into bite-size pieces	375 g
1 tbsp	vegetable oil *or* olive oil	15 mL
4	thin slices ginger root	4
3	anchovies, finely chopped	3
2	green onions, cut into short lengths	2
1	clove garlic, minced	1
1	small bay leaf	1
1	stalk lemon grass (optional), bruised with the back of knife and cut into 2-inch (5 cm) lengths	1
2	cloves (optional)	2
1	green finger chili, split, seeded and cut into pieces	1
4 cups	chicken broth	1 L
1	large green or semi-ripe tomato, cut into very thin wedges	1
1/4 cup	lemon juice	50 mL
1/4 tsp	sugar	1 mL
	Salt to taste	
	Coriander leaves *or* chopped parsley for garnish (optional)	

1. In a small pot of boiling water, blanch lemon peel for 10 seconds; drain, reserving the peel.

2. In a bowl combine cornstarch and pepper. Toss chicken pieces with cornstarch mixture.

3. In a heavy-bottomed saucepan, heat oil over medium-high heat. Add ginger, anchovies, green onions, garlic, bay leaf and, if using, lemon grass and cloves; cook until ingredients start to become fragrant. Add the chicken and chili pieces; cook, stirring frequently, to sear the chicken. Reduce heat slightly and continue cooking

1 to 2 minutes, but without browning the chicken. Add lemon peel and broth; bring to a boil. Add green tomato and reduce heat to simmer. Cook a few more minutes until the chicken pieces are thoroughly cooked but not dry. Add lemon juice and sugar; cook 30 seconds. Season to taste with salt. Serve garnished with coriander or parsley, if desired.

Variations

- For a slightly richer flavor, marinate the chicken pieces (before dredging) in 1 tbsp (15 mL) brandy and 1 tsp (5 mL) lemon juice for 20 minutes.

- If you are growing chilies in your vegetable garden, pick about a dozen leaves from the top of the plant and add to the soup just before the lemon. Chili leaves are not spicy and have a nice herbal flavor that is great in chicken soup. If you use them, omit the coriander or parsley garnish.

Serves 6

TIP

Bok choy, napa, or Chinese cabbage can be used. Otherwise, substitute romaine lettuce.

•

Leeks can have a lot of hidden dirt — to clean thoroughly, slice in half lengthwise and wash under cold running water, getting between the layers where dirt hides.

•

Any canned beans can replace red kidney beans.

•

If green beans are unavailable, substitute chopped broccoli or zucchini.

MAKE AHEAD

Prepare soup up to a day in advance, but leave Step 2 until just before serving.

FROM
ROSE REISMAN'S
ENLIGHTENED
HOME COOKING

Vegetable Bean Chicken Soup

2 tsp	vegetable oil	10 mL
1 1/2 tsp	minced garlic	7 mL
3/4 cup	chopped onions	175 mL
1 cup	chopped leeks	250 mL
1 cup	chopped carrots	250 mL
5 cups	chicken stock	1.25 L
1 1/4 cups	peeled, chopped potatoes	300 mL
2	bay leaves	2
1/2 tsp	dried basil	2 mL
1/2 tsp	dried oregano	2 mL
2 cups	chopped bok choy	500 mL
1 cup	drained canned red kidney beans	250 mL
1 cup	trimmed green beans	250 mL
6 oz	skinless, boneless chicken breast, cut into 1/2-inch (1 cm) cubes	150 g
1/3 cup	chopped fresh parsley	75 mL
1/4 tsp	ground black pepper	1 mL

1. In a nonstick saucepan sprayed with vegetable spray, heat oil over medium heat. Add garlic, onions, leeks and carrots; cook 4 minutes or until onions are softened, stirring occasionally. Add stock, potatoes, bay leaves, basil and oregano; bring to a boil. Cover, reduce heat to low and simmer for 20 minutes or until potatoes are tender.

2. Stir in bok choy, kidney beans, green beans and chicken. Cover and cook for 5 minutes or until chicken is just done. Stir in parsley and pepper and serve.

Salads

Chicken and Vegetable Salad with Chinese Sesame Sauce

Serves 3 or 4

This ever-popular salad can serve as an appetizer, a shared course in an Asian meal or a main course for lunch or a light dinner. Doubled or tripled in quantity, it also makes an excellent buffet dish. With careful cutting and arranging of the vegetables and garnishes, an attractive and lively presentation can grace any table.

The recipe here calls for a poached chicken breast, but grilled or even cold left-over roasted chicken will work well. For a tastier and more economical poached chicken breast, purchase a bone-in breast with the skin. The bones and the skin will help the chicken to retain flavor while poaching and can be removed for the salad. The resulting poaching liquid can also be used as a light chicken broth in other dishes.

FROM
THE ASIAN BISTRO COOKBOOK BY ANDREW CHASE

Sesame Sauce

1 1/2 tsp	hot mustard powder	7 mL
1/4 cup	sesame paste *or* peanut butter	50 mL
1 tbsp	sesame oil (or 2 tbsp [25 mL] if using peanut butter)	15 mL
4 tsp	vinegar, preferably rice vinegar	20 mL
2 tsp	soya sauce	10 mL
1 tsp	minced garlic	5 mL
1 tsp	granulated sugar	5 mL
1/2 tsp	fish sauce (optional)	2 mL
1/4 tsp	white pepper	1 mL
1/4 tsp	salt	1 mL

Salad

1/4 tsp	salt	1 mL
1	stalk celery	1
10	black peppercorns	10
4	slices ginger root	4
2	green onions; 1 whole, 1 finely sliced	2
1	stalk coriander (optional)	1
1	chicken breast (with bones and skin)	1
	Napa cabbage *or* lettuce leaves (3 or 4), cut into large shred	
1	2-inch (5 cm) daikon radish *or* 6 red radishes, sliced	1
1	3-inch (7.5 cm) piece cucumber, sliced	1
1	green finger chili, sliced into rings	1
1 tbsp	finely chopped red bell pepper	15 mL
1 tbsp	coriander leaves	15 mL
1 tsp	toasted white sesame seeds for garnish (optional)	5 mL
1 tsp	toasted black sesame seeds for garnish (optional)	5 mL

1. Prepare the sauce: Add enough cold water to the mustard powder to make a thin paste; let stand 10 minutes.

In a food processor combine mustard paste, sesame paste, sesame oil, vinegar, soya sauce, garlic, sugar, fish sauce (if using), pepper and salt; purée until smooth. Add enough cold water to make a thick but pourable sauce. (The sauce can be refrigerated for 5 days; bring to room temperature before using).

2. Bring 3 cups (750 mL) water and salt to a boil. Blanch celery 30 seconds; remove, rinse in cold water, cut diagonally into bite-size pieces and set aside. Add peppercorns, ginger, whole green onion and coriander, if using, to the boiling water. Add chicken breast, skin-side up; when water returns to a boil, reduce heat to low, cover and cook 12 to 15 minutes or until chicken is cooked through but still moist. Remove from water; cool. Strain liquid and save for use as a light stock. Remove and discard skin and bones; shred chicken meat or slice thinly.

3. Line serving platter with Napa cabbage leaves; cover with radish and cucumber, then celery and chicken. Drizzle sauce in lines over the salad. Sprinkle with chili, red pepper, coriander and, if desired, sesame seeds.

Variations

- Some northern Chinese and, especially, Koreans prefer a sauce with a pronounced mustard taste and sinus-clearing piquancy. For this, make sure you use hot English mustard powder. Or, for the best and hottest mustard powder, buy the Korean product at Korean grocers. Avoid Chinese mustard powder, as it is inferior to the English variety. Increase the mustard to 1 tbsp (15 mL).

- *Wasabi*, Japanese green horseradish, can also replace the hot mustard. Use 2 tsp (10 mL) powdered *wasabi* and add enough cold water to make a thick paste; let it sit covered 10 minutes before adding to the sauce.

- If you ever see fresh radish sprouts at your grocers, buy them for this salad. The attractive sprouts are absolutely delicious and have the tangy flavor of radish. Onion sprouts can replace the green onion in the salad. Chopped pickled young ginger also makes for a very nice garnish.

Chicken Salad with Tarragon and Pecans

Serves 4

TIP

If tarragon is unavailable, substitute 1/4 cup (50 mL) chopped fresh dill.

•

Fresh tuna or swordfish are delicious substitutes for chicken.

•

Toast pecans in small skillet on medium heat until browned, 2 to 3 minutes.

MAKE AHEAD

Prepare and refrigerate salad and dressing separately early in day, but do not mix until ready to serve.

FROM
ROSE REISMAN BRINGS
HOME LIGHT COOKING

10 oz	boneless skinless chicken breast, cubed	300 g
3/4 cup	chopped sweet red or green peppers	175 mL
3/4 cup	chopped carrots	175 mL
3/4 cup	chopped broccoli florets	175 mL
3/4 cup	chopped snow peas	175 mL
3/4 cup	chopped red onions	175 mL
1 tbsp	chopped pecans, toasted	15 mL

Dressing

1/2 cup	2% yogurt	125 mL
2 tbsp	lemon juice	25 mL
2 tbsp	light mayonnaise	25 mL
1 tsp	crushed garlic	5 mL
1 tsp	Dijon mustard	5 mL
1/4 cup	chopped fresh parsley	50 mL
2 tsp	dried tarragon (or 3 tbsp [45 mL] chopped fresh)	10 mL
	Salt and pepper	

1. In small saucepan, bring 2 cups (500 mL) water to boil; reduce heat to simmer. Add chicken; cover and cook just until no longer pink inside, 2 to 4 minutes. Drain and place in serving bowl.

2. Add red pepper, carrot, broccoli, snow peas and onion; toss well.

3. Dressing: In a small bowl, combine yogurt, lemon juice, mayonnaise, garlic, mustard, parsley, tarragon, and salt and pepper to taste; pour over chicken and mix well. Taste and adjust seasoning. Sprinkle with pecans.

Serves 6

Oriental Chicken Salad with Mandarin Oranges, Snow Peas and Asparagus

TIP

Replace chicken with shrimp, pork or steak.

•

Broccoli or green beans can replace asparagus.

•

Thinly sliced carrots (julienned) can replace bean sprouts.

MAKE AHEAD

Prepare salad and dressing early in the day, keeping separate until ready to serve. Dressing can keep for days.

FROM
**ROSE REISMAN'S
ENLIGHTENED
HOME COOKING**

12 oz	skinless boneless chicken breasts	375 g
1 cup	asparagus cut into 1-inch (2.5 cm) pieces	250 mL
1 1/4 cups	halved snow peas	300 mL
1 cup	sliced baby corn cobs	250 mL
1 cup	bean sprouts	250 mL
1 cup	canned mandarin oranges, drained	250 mL
1 1/2 cups	sliced red or green peppers	375 mL
3/4 cup	sliced water chestnuts	175 mL
2	medium green onions, chopped	2

Dressing

2 tbsp	orange juice concentrate, thawed	25 mL
1 tbsp	rice wine vinegar	15 mL
1 tbsp	soya sauce	15 mL
2 tsp	honey	10 mL
2 tsp	vegetable oil	10 mL
1 tsp	sesame oil	5 mL
1 tsp	minced ginger root	5 mL
1 tsp	minced garlic	5 mL

1. In a nonstick skillet sprayed with vegetable spray, sauté chicken breasts and cook approximately 7 minutes, or until browned on both sides and just done at center. Let chicken cool, then cut into 1/2-inch (1 cm) cubes and place in large serving bowl.

2. In boiling water or microwave, blanch asparagus for 2 minutes or until tender-crisp; refresh in cold water and drain. As well, cook snow peas for 45 seconds or until tender-crisp; refresh in cold water and drain. Place in serving bowl with chicken. Add baby corn, bean sprouts, mandarin oranges, red peppers, water chestnuts and green onions to bowl and toss.

3. In a small bowl, whisk together orange juice concentrate, vinegar, soya sauce, honey, vegetable oil, sesame oil, ginger and garlic; pour over salad and toss.

Warm Chicken Salad with Orange Dressing

1 1/2 cups	snow peas, sliced in half	375 mL
8 oz	boneless skinless chicken breasts, cubed	250 g
1	large head romaine lettuce, torn	1
1 cup	mandarin orange segments	250 mL
1/2 cup	sliced water chestnuts	125 mL
2 tbsp	pecans	25 mL

Dressing

2 tsp	grated orange rind	10 mL
1/4 cup	orange juice	50 mL
1/2 tsp	crushed garlic	2 mL
1 tbsp	frozen orange juice concentrate, thawed	15 mL
2 tbsp	light mayonnaise	25 mL
3 tbsp	vegetable oil	45 mL
1 tbsp	chopped fresh tarragon (or 1 tsp [5 mL] dried)	15 mL

1. Dressing: In a small bowl, whisk together orange rind and juice, garlic, orange juice concentrate, mayonnaise, oil and tarragon until well blended. Set aside.

2. Steam or microwave snow peas just until tender-crisp. Drain and place in salad bowl.

3. In a saucepan pour in just enough water to cover chicken; bring to boil. Reduce heat, cover and simmer for 2 to 3 minutes or until no longer pink; drain and add to snow peas.

4. Add lettuce, oranges and chestnuts to salad bowl. Pour dressing over top and toss. Sprinkle with pecans.

S e r v e s   4

This is a tasty way to stretch leftover roast chicken or turkey. In fact, roast beef or pork will do just as well.

FROM
NEW WORLD NOODLES BY BILL JONES & STEPHEN WONG

Shredded Chicken Salad with Spicy Sesame Vinaigrette

Dressing

2 tbsp	honey	25 mL
1 tbsp	Worcestershire sauce	15 mL
1 1/2 cups	SPICY SESAME VINAIGRETTE (see recipe, next page)	375 mL

Salad

2 cups	bean sprouts (preferably mung bean)	500 mL
2 tbsp	vegetable oil	25 mL
3	cloves garlic, peeled and very thinly sliced lengthwise	3
1 lb	Chinese-style steamed noodles *or* 8 oz (250 g) dried fettuccine	500 g
1 cup	English cucumber cut into thin matchsticks	250 mL
1 cup	carrots, cut into thin matchsticks	250 mL
2 cups	cooked chicken, beef or pork cut into julienne strips	500 mL
1/2 cup	thinly sliced green onions, green parts only	125 mL
2 tbsp	sesame seeds	25 mL

1. In a small bowl or pot, combine all dressing ingredients and mix well. (If necessary, warm dressing over low heat or in microwave to ensure honey is dissolved.)

2. In a large bowl of ice water, refresh bean sprouts for 15 minutes until crisp. Drain and set aside.

3. In a small skillet, heat oil over medium heat for 30 seconds. Add garlic and fry until golden, about 2 minutes. (Be careful not to let it burn.) With a slotted spoon, transfer garlic to a paper towel. Reserve oil.

4. In a large pot of boiling salted water, blanch noodles for 1 minute. Drain and, using chopsticks or two forks, toss to dry. (If using pasta, prepare according to package directions.) Transfer to large salad bowl, toss with reserved garlic oil and allow to cool.

5. Add bean sprouts, cucumber, carrots, chicken and green onions. Pour dressing evenly over salad; toss well. Sprinkle with sesame seeds and serve immediately.

Spicy Sesame Vinaigrette

**Makes about
1 1/2 cups**

(375 mL)

The sauce will keep, covered and refrigerated, for up to 3 days.

•

This is a classic dipping sauce for Chinese dumplings but it also works well with steamed prawns, crab or even fresh oysters.

1/2 cup	soya sauce	125 mL
1/2 cup	Chinese red vinegar *or* balsamic vinegar	125 mL
1 tbsp	chili oil *or* 1 or 2 jalapeno peppers, thinly sliced	15 mL
1 tbsp	sesame oil	15 mL
1 tbsp	minced ginger root	15 mL
2 tbsp	water *or* chicken stock	25 mL

1. In a small bowl, combine all ingredients. Set aside for 30 minutes to develop flavors. Serve at room temperature as a dipping sauce or a dressing for seafood.

Chicken and Asparagus Salad with Lemon Dill Vinaigrette

TIP

Containing both protein and carbohydrates, this salad is a complete meal.

•

Substitute broccoli or fresh green beans for the asparagus.

FROM
ROSE REISMAN BRINGS
HOME LIGHT COOKING

Salad

12	baby red potatoes (or 4 small white potatoes)	12
8 oz	boneless skinless chicken breasts, cubed	250 g
1/4 cup	water	50 mL
1/4 cup	white wine	50 mL
8 oz	asparagus, trimmed and cut into small pieces	250 g
2	small heads Boston lettuce, torn into pieces	2

Lemon Dill Vinaigrette

3 tbsp	balsamic vinegar	45 mL
2 tbsp	lemon juice	25 mL
1 tbsp	water	15 mL
1	large green onion, minced	1
3/4 tsp	garlic	4 mL
2 tbsp	chopped fresh dill (or 1 tsp [5 mL] dried dillweed)	25 mL
3 tbsp	olive oil	45 mL

1. In a saucepan of boiling water, cook potatoes until just tender. Peel and cut into cubes. Place in salad bowl and set aside.

2. In a saucepan bring chicken, water and wine to boil; reduce heat, cover and simmer for approximately 2 minutes or until chicken is no longer pink. Drain and add to potatoes in bowl.

3. Steam or microwave asparagus until just tender-crisp; drain and add to bowl. Add lettuce.

4. Lemon Dill Vinaigrette: In a bowl whisk together vinegar, lemon juice, water, onion, garlic and dill; whisk in oil until combined. Pour over chicken mixture; toss to coat well.

Chicken Tarragon Pasta Salad

12 oz	rotini *or* fusilli	375 g
12 oz	skinless boneless chicken breasts, cut into 1-inch (2.5 cm) cubes	375 g
1 1/2 cups	chopped broccoli	375 mL
1/2 cup	diced carrots	125 mL
1 1/2 cups	diced red peppers	375 mL
3/4 cup	diced green peppers	175 mL
1/2 cup	diced red onions	125 mL

Dressing

1/2 cup	2% yogurt	125 mL
1/3 cup	light mayonnaise	75 mL
3 tbsp	lemon juice	45 mL
1/3 cup	chopped fresh tarragon *or* dill (or 3 tsp [15 mL] dried)	75 mL
2 1/2 tbsp	honey	35 mL
2 tsp	crushed garlic	10 mL
1 1/2 tsp	Dijon mustard	7 mL

1. Cook pasta in boiling water according to package instructions or until firm to the bite. Rinse with cold water. Drain and place in serving bowl.

2. In a nonstick skillet sprayed with vegetable spray, sauté chicken until no longer pink, approximately 3 minutes. Cool. Add to pasta.

3. Blanch broccoli and carrots in boiling water just until tender, approximately 3 minutes. Drain and refresh with cold water; add to pasta. Add red and green peppers and onions.

4. Make the dressing: In a small bowl, combine yogurt, mayonnaise, lemon juice, tarragon, honey, garlic and mustard until mixed. Pour over pasta, and toss.

Chicken and Rice Salad with Creamy Garlic Dressing

2 cups	cubed cooked chicken	500 mL
3/4 cup	cooked rice (preferably brown)	175 mL
1/3 cup	bran cereal*	75 mL
1/2 cup	thinly sliced celery	125 mL
1/2 cup	thinly sliced sweet red pepper	125 mL
1/4 cup	sliced green onions	50 mL
3 cups	finely chopped bok choy or nappa cabbage	750 mL
1/2 cup	CREAMY GARLIC DRESSING	125 mL

★ *Use a wheat bran breakfast cereal.*

1. In a large serving bowl, combine chicken, rice, cereal, celery, red pepper, onions and bok choy. Toss with CREAMY GARLIC DRESSING (recipe follows).

Creamy Garlic Dressing

1/3 cup	2% cottage cheese	75 mL
1 tsp	crushed garlic	5 mL
3 tbsp	lemon juice	45 mL
2 tbsp	vegetable oil	25 mL
2 tbsp	water	25 mL
2 tbsp	light mayonnaise	25 mL
2 tbsp	grated Parmesan cheese	25 mL

1. In a food processor combine cottage cheese, garlic, lemon juice, oil, water, mayonnaise and Parmesan; process until smooth.

Main Dishes

Roasted Chicken with Apricot Orange Glaze and Couscous Stuffing

Serves 4 to 6

TIP

Couscous stuffing is a great dish to accompany other meals.

•

Follow the instructions carefully for the apricot glaze. Glaze half the chicken without added cornstarch, the other half with cornstarch. The extra glaze serves as gravy.

•

Do not stuff chicken until ready to bake; this will avoid bacterial contamination.

MAKE AHEAD

The glaze and couscous can be prepared earlier in the day.

FROM
ROSE REISMAN'S
ENLIGHTENED
HOME COOKING

PREHEAT OVEN TO 400° F (200° C)
ROASTING PAN WITH RACK

3 lb	roasting chicken	1.5 kg

Couscous Stuffing

1 tbsp	orange juice concentrate, thawed	15 mL
1 tbsp	chopped fresh coriander *or* parsley	15 mL
2 tsp	hoisin sauce	10 mL
1 1/2 tsp	honey	7 mL
1 tsp	minced garlic	5 mL
1/2 tsp	minced ginger root	2 mL
1 tsp	sesame oil	5 mL
1 tsp	vegetable oil	5 mL
1 3/4 cups	chicken stock	425 mL
1 cup	couscous	250 mL
1 cup	chopped snow peas	250 mL
2/3 cup	chopped red onions	150 mL
1/2 cup	chopped carrots	125 mL
1/2 cup	chopped dried apricots	125 mL

Apricot Glaze

3/4 cup	apricot or peach jam	175 mL
1/2 cup	chicken stock	125 mL
3 tbsp	orange juice concentrate, thawed	45 mL
1 tbsp	soya sauce	15 mL
1 tsp	minced garlic	5 mL
1 tsp	minced ginger root	5 mL
1 tbsp	cornstarch	15 mL
1 cup	chicken stock	250 mL

1. Stuffing: In aa small bowl, whisk together orange juice concentrate, coriander, hoisin, honey, garlic, ginger, sesame oil and vegetable oil; set aside. Bring stock to a boil in saucepan; stir in couscous, cover and remove from heat. Let stand for 5 minutes; fluff with a fork. In a bowl combine couscous, snow peas, red onions, carrots, dried apricots and orange juice sauce.

2. Loosely stuff chicken with some of the couscous stuffing. Place on rack in roasting pan sprayed with vegetable spray. Put remaining couscous stuffing in a casserole dish and cover. Set aside.

3. Glaze: In a bowl whisk together apricot jam, stock, orange juice concentrate, soya sauce, garlic and ginger. Measure out 1/2 cup (125 mL) of the glaze; combine with cornstarch and 1/2 cup (125 mL) of the chicken stock and set aside. Pour remaining 1/2 cup (125 mL) chicken stock into roasting pan under chicken. Spread some of the remaining apricot glaze (without corn-starch) over chicken; bake for 1 hour, or until juices run clear when leg is pierced at thickest point. Baste chicken with apricot glaze every 15 minutes as it roasts. Put casserole with stuffing in oven for last 30 minutes of roasting time. Let chicken rest for 10 minutes before carving.

4. Meanwhile, remove juices, if any, from roasting pan and place in saucepan. Add reserved apricot glaze-cornstarch mixture; heat over medium heat for 2 minutes or until slightly thickened. Serve chicken with sauce and stuffing. Remove skin before eating.

Chicken Breasts Stuffed with Spinach and Cheese with Tomato Garlic Sauce

PREHEAT OVEN TO 400° F (200° C)
BAKING DISH SPRAYED WITH VEGETABLE SPRAY

4	boneless skinless chicken breasts	4
1 1/2 tsp	vegetable oil	7 mL
1/2 tsp	crushed garlic	2 mL
1	medium green onion, finely chopped	1
1/4 cup	drained cooked chopped spinach	50 mL
1/4 cup	diced mushrooms	50 mL
1/4 cup	shredded mozzarella cheese	50 mL
1/4 cup	chicken stock	50 mL

Sauce

1 1/2 tsp	margarine *or* butter	7 mL
1 tsp	crushed garlic	5 mL
1 1/2 cups	diced tomatoes	375 mL
1/3 cup	chicken stock	75 mL
1 tbsp	chopped fresh parsley	15 mL

1. Place chicken between 2 sheets of waxed paper; pound until flattened. Set aside.

2. In a nonstick skillet, heat oil; sauté garlic, onion, spinach and mushrooms until softened. Spoon evenly over breasts; sprinkle with cheese. Roll up and fasten with toothpicks.

3. Place chicken in baking dish; pour in stock. Cover and bake for 10 minutes or until chicken is no longer pink. Remove chicken to serving dish and keep warm.

4. Sauce: Meanwhile, in a small saucepan, melt margarine; sauté garlic for 1 minute. Stir in tomatoes and chicken stock; cook for 3 minutes or until heated through. Add parsley and serve over chicken.

Chicken Kabobs with Ginger Lemon Marinade

8 oz	boneless skinless chicken breasts, cut into 2-inch (5 cm) cubes	250 g
16	squares sweet green pepper	16
16	pineapple chunks (fresh or canned)	16
16	cherry tomatoes	16

Ginger Lemon Marinade

3 tbsp	lemon juice	45 mL
2 tbsp	water	25 mL
1 tbsp	vegetable oil	15 mL
2 tsp	sesame oil	10 mL
1 1/2 tsp	red wine vinegar	7 mL
4 tsp	brown sugar	20 mL
1 tsp	minced gingerroot (or 1/4 tsp [1 mL] ground)	5 mL
1/2 tsp	ground coriander	2 mL
1/2 tsp	ground fennel seeds (optional)	2 mL

1. Ginger Lemon Marinade: In a small bowl, combine lemon juice, water, vegetable oil, sesame oil, vinegar, brown sugar, ginger, coriander, and fennel seeds (if using); mix well. Add chicken and mix well; marinate for 20 minutes.

2. Alternately thread chicken cubes, green pepper, pineapple and tomatoes onto 4 long or 8 short barbecue skewers. Barbecue for 15 to 20 minutes or just until chicken is no longer pink inside, brushing often with marinade and rotating every 5 minutes.

Sautéed Rice with Almonds, Curry and Ginger

Serves 4

TIP

Other raw vegetables can replace the red pepper and snow peas. Try chopped broccoli or sliced zucchini.

•

If bok choy or nappa cabbage is unavailable, use sliced romaine or iceberg lettuce. Bok choy and nappa cabbage can be bought at Asian markets or found in the produce section of some supermarkets.

•

Toast almonds in skillet on top of stove or in 400° F (200° C) oven for 2 minutes.

MAKE AHEAD

Prepare and refrigerate early in day. Just prior to serving, reheat on low heat.

FROM
ROSE REISMAN
BRINGS HOME LIGHT
COOKING

1 tbsp	vegetable oil	15 mL
1 tsp	crushed garlic	5 mL
1 1/2 cups	thinly sliced bok choy or nappa cabbage	375 mL
1 cup	snow peas	250 mL
1/2 cup	chopped sweet red pepper	125 mL
1/3 cup	chopped carrot	75 mL
1 tsp	ground ginger	5 mL
1 tsp	curry powder	5 mL
3/4 cup	chicken stock	175 mL
4 tsp	soya sauce	20 mL
1	egg	1
2 cups	cooked rice	500 mL
2 tbsp	toasted chopped almonds	25 mL
2 tbsp	chopped green onion	25 mL

1. In large nonstick skillet, heat oil; sauté garlic, cabbage, snow peas, red pepper and carrot for 3 minutes or just until tender, stirring constantly. Add ginger, curry powder, stock and soya sauce; cook for 1 minute.

2. Add egg and rice; cook for 1 minute or until egg is well incorporated. Place in serving dish and sprinkle with almonds and green onions.

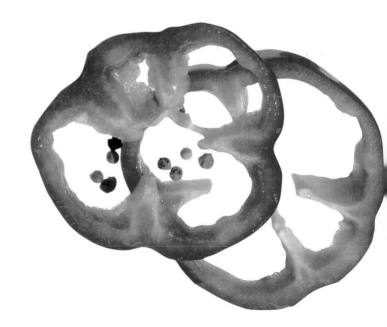

Chicken Tetrazzini

PREHEAT BROILER

8 oz	spaghetti	250 g
4 tsp	margarine *or* butter	20 mL
1 1/2 tsp	crushed garlic	7 mL
1 cup	chopped onions	250 mL
1 cup	chopped sweet red peppers	250 mL
1 cup	sliced mushrooms	250 mL
3 tbsp	all-purpose flour	45 mL
1 1/2 cups	chicken stock	375 mL
1 cup	2% milk	250 mL
3 tbsp	white wine	45 mL
1 1/2 tsp	Dijon mustard	7 mL
4 oz	cooked boneless skinless chicken pieces	125 g
1/2 cup	shredded Cheddar cheese	125 mL
1 tbsp	grated Parmesan cheese	15 mL
	Chopped fresh parsley	

1. In a saucepan of boiling water, cook spaghetti according to package directions or until firm to the bite; drain.

2. Meanwhile, in a nonstick saucepan, melt margarine; sauté garlic, onion, red pepper and mushrooms until softened, approximately 5 minutes. Add flour and cook, stirring, for 1 minute.

3. Add stock, milk, wine and mustard; cook, stirring, for 3 minutes or until thickened. Add chicken.

4. Add sauce to spaghetti and toss to mix well; place in baking dish. Sprinkle Cheddar and Parmesan cheeses over top; bake until top is golden, approximately 5 minutes. Garnish with parsley.

Roasted Chicken with Asian Glaze and Fruit Sauce

Serves 4

TIP

This glaze can also be used over Cornish hens or game birds.

•

Substitute dried prunes or raisins for the dates or apricots for a change.

FROM
ROSE REISMAN BRINGS HOME LIGHT COOKING

PREHEAT OVEN TO 400° F (200° C)

1	whole chicken (2 1/2 to 3 lbs [1.25 to 1.5 kg])	1

Glaze

1 tsp	crushed garlic	5 mL
1 tsp	minced gingerroot (or 1/4 tsp [1 mL] ground ginger)	5 mL
1/4 cup	honey	50 mL
1/4 cup	sweet dessert wine (plum wine)	50 mL
Pinch	chili flakes	Pinch
1 tbsp	margarine, melted	15 mL
Pinch	dried coriander and/or cumin	Pinch
	Salt and pepper	
1/2 cup	chicken stock	125 mL

Sauce

1 tbsp	cornstarch	15 mL
1/2 cup	chicken stock	125 mL
1/4 cup	chopped dates	50 mL
1/4 cup	chopped dried apricots	50 mL

1. Place chicken in roasting pan.

2. Glaze: In a small bowl, mix together garlic, ginger, honey, wine, chili flakes, margarine, coriander, salt and pepper to taste and stock; set half aside for sauce. Brush some of the remaining mixture over chicken. Bake for 50 to 60 minutes or until meat thermometer registers 185° F (85° C), basting with more honey mixture every 15 minutes.

3. Cut chicken into 4 quarters; place on serving dish and keep warm.

4. Sauce: Pour reserved honey mixture into small saucepan; stir in cornstarch, mixing well. Add chicken stock along with dates and apricots; cook over medium heat, stirring, for 2 minutes or until thickened. Pour over chicken. Remove skin before eating.

Almond Chicken Breasts with Creamy Tarragon Mustard Sauce

Serves 4

1 lb	skinless, boneless chicken breasts	500 g
3 tbsp	all-purpose flour	45 mL
1	egg white	1
3 tbsp	water	45 mL
1/3 cup	finely chopped almonds	75 mL
1/2 cup	seasoned bread crumbs	125 mL
2 tsp	vegetable oil	10 mL

Sauce

1/4 cup	light mayonnaise	50 mL
1/4 cup	light sour cream	50 mL
1 tsp	Dijon mustard	5 mL
1 tsp	dried tarragon	5 mL

1. Between sheets of waxed paper, pound breasts to 1/4-inch (5 mm) thickness. Dust with flour. In shallow bowl, whisk together egg white and water. Combine almonds and bread crumbs and place on a plate.

2. In a nonstick skillet sprayed with vegetable spray, heat oil over medium-high heat. Dip breasts in egg wash, then in crumb mixture. Cook for 3 minutes on one side; turn and cook for 2 minutes longer or until just done at center.

3. Meanwhile, in a small saucepan, whisk together mayonnaise, sour cream, mustard and tarragon; heat over low heat just until warm. Serve over chicken.

Chicken Breasts Stuffed with Brie Cheese, Red Pepper and Green Onions

TIP

Instead of serving each breast whole, slice each crosswise into medallions and fan out on plates.

•

Replace chicken with turkey, veal or pork scallopini.

•

Brie is a high-fat cheese, but 2 oz (50 g) divided among 4 servings makes it acceptable.

MAKE AHEAD

Prepare chicken breasts early in the day, sauté, then refrigerate. Bake for an extra 5 minutes just prior to serving.

FROM
ROSE REISMAN'S
ENLIGHTENED HOME
COOKING

PREHEAT OVEN TO 425° F (220° C)
BAKING SHEET SPRAYED WITH VEGETABLE SPRAY

2 oz	Brie cheese, at room temperature	50 g
3 tbsp	finely chopped red peppers	45 mL
3 tbsp	finely chopped green onions (about 2 medium)	45 mL
1 tsp	minced garlic	5 mL
1	egg	1
2 tbsp	2% milk	25 mL
1/2 cup	seasoned bread crumbs	125 mL
1 lb	skinless boneless chicken breasts (about 4)	500 g
1 tbsp	vegetable oil	15 mL

1. In a small bowl, mix Brie, red peppers, green onions and garlic. In small bowl whisk together egg and milk. Put bread crumbs on a plate.

2. Between sheets of waxed paper, pound breasts to 1/4-inch (5 mm) thickness. Put 1 tbsp (15 mL) Brie mixture at a short end of each breast. Roll up tightly; secure edge with a toothpick.

3. Dip each chicken roll in egg wash, then in bread crumbs. Heat oil in large nonstick skillet sprayed with vegetable spray, cook over high heat for 3 minutes, turning often, or until browned on all sides. Put on prepared baking sheet and bake for 10 minutes or until just done at centre. Remove toothpicks before serving.

Stir-Fried Chicken with Peaches and Pickled Ginger

Serves 4

In this recipe, the sweetness of the peaches strikes a wonderful balance with the peppery bean paste and the slightly tart pickled ginger. Although canned peaches work very well, feel free to use fresh peaches in season. Peel peaches as you would a tomato by dipping them in boiling water for about 30 seconds.

FROM
NEW WORLD CHINESE COOKING BY BILL JONES & STEPHEN WONG

Marinade

2 tbsp	soya sauce	25 mL
1/4 tsp	salt	1 mL
Pinch	white pepper	Pinch
2 tsp	cornstarch	10 mL
12 oz	boneless skinless chicken breast, thinly sliced	375 g

Sauce

2 tbsp	pickled ginger liquid	25 mL
1 tbsp	ketchup	15 mL
1 tsp	hot bean paste	5 mL
2 tbsp	chicken stock	25 mL
1 tbsp	vegetable oil	15 mL
1/2 cup	roasted cashews	125 mL
12	slices pickled ginger, cut into thin strips	12
1 tsp	minced garlic	5 mL
2	stalks celery, cut diagonally into thin strips	2
1 1/2 cups	sliced canned peaches	375 mL
	Salt, pepper and sugar to taste	

1. In a bowl combine ingredients for marinade. Add chicken; mix well. Marinate for 30 minutes.

2. In a small bowl, combine ingredients for sauce; set aside.

3. In a wok or nonstick skillet, heat oil over medium-high heat for 30 seconds. Add cashews and fry until golden brown and crispy, about 1 minute. Remove with slotted spoon and set aside.

Vietnamese Lemon Grass Grilled Chicken

Serves 4

The Vietnamese — as well as Cambodians, Laotians and, to a lesser degree, Thais — are especially fond of thick, fermented fish sauces. Unlike regular fish sauce, which is the salty water that comes to the top of a pot of fermenting salted fish, these sauces also include the flesh of the fish. Although they pack quite a stench, they imbue a delicate flavor to foods. In Vietnam, the most common one is called Mam Nem. It can be used as the base for a marinade. It is available at some Southeast Asian and Chinese grocers, but most of us will have to make do with fish sauce or anchovies to flavor the chicken. If you do find it, however, use 3 tbsp (45 mL) to replace the fish sauce. Use caution when opening the sauce bottle: If it has sat too long on the shelf, the fermentation may cause it to spew malodorous sauce all over your kitchen with explosive force — an event I unfortunately have experienced in my Swiss mother's immaculately clean kitchen.

BAKING SHEET

1	chicken (3 to 4 lbs, 1.5 to 2 kg)	1
3 tbsp	fish sauce *or* 8 anchovies mixed in 3 tbsp (45 mL) water	45 mL
1 tbsp	grated lime rind	15 mL
3 tbsp	lime juice	45 mL
1 tbsp	chopped fresh galangal *or* 1 tsp (5 mL) galangal powder (optional)	15 mL
2 tsp	minced ginger root	10 mL
6	cloves garlic	6
2	stalks lemon grass, very finely chopped	2
1	green onion *or* 2 small shallots, chopped	1
1 1/2 tsp	brown sugar	20 mL
1 tsp	black pepper	15 mL
3/4 tsp	cayenne pepper	4 mL
3/4 tsp	ground fennel	4 mL
1/2 tsp	ground cumin	2 mL
1/4 tsp	ground cloves	1 mL
2 tbsp	vegetable oil	25 mL
	Lime wedges	

1. Halve the whole chicken by cutting through the breast bone, opening the chicken up and cutting out the back bone (keep it for stock).

2. In a blender combine the fish sauce, lime rind and juice, galangal (if using), ginger root, garlic, lemon grass and green onions; chop as finely as possible. Mix in sugar, pepper, cayenne, fennel, cumin and cloves. Rub mixture over both sides of the chicken; place in a shallow glass dish, cover with plastic wrap and refrigerate overnight or up to 3 days.

3. Bring chicken to room temperature. Preheat oven to 375° F (190° C). Shake most of the marinade off chicken; lay chicken skin-side up on baking sheet. Pour

FROM
THE ASIAN BISTRO
COOKBOOK BY
ANDREW CHASE

oil over skin. Bake 40 minutes. Remove the chicken from the oven and either turn on the broiler or prepare the grill or barbecue. Brush some of the oil from the baking tray over the chicken and broil on the middle rack or grill over medium heat on both sides until the skin is crispy and the other side is nicely browned. (The baking can be done some hours ahead as the grilling or broiling will reheat it through.) Serve with lime wedges and chili sauce.

Variation

- The chicken can be left whole, marinated and roasted in a 375° F (190° C) oven for 1 1/2 hours. Start it breast down on a well-oiled roasting pan. Turn the bird around after 50 minutes and then baste every 10 minutes with the oil from the bottom of the pan to ensure a crispy skin.

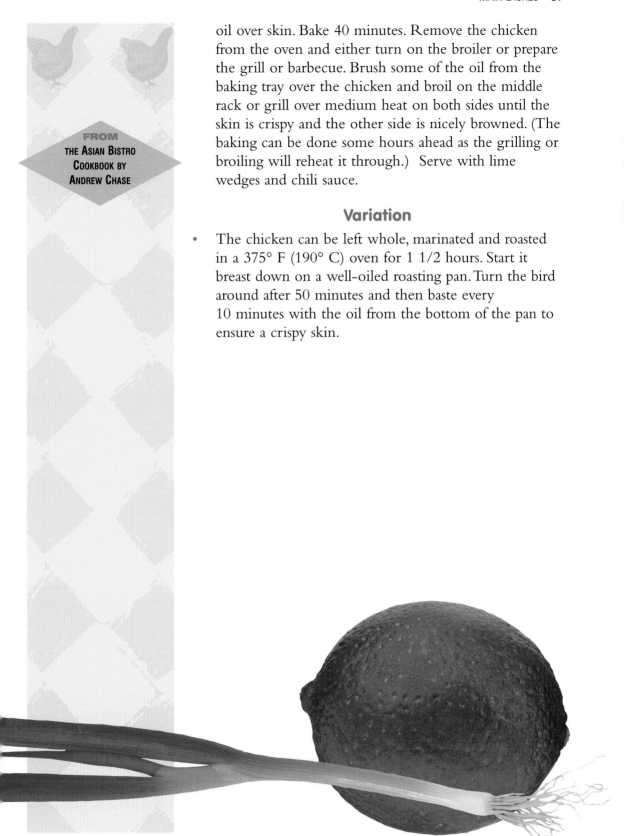

Peking Savory Fried Cornish Hens

Serves 4

This dish might seem a bit complicated — after all, the chicken is marinated, steamed and then fried — but this time-honored Chinese method of cooking poultry is really quite simple and well worth the effort. The marinating and steaming allow the savory spicing to permeate the flesh of the hens, and the final frying crisps the skin. This method also provides the advantage of being able to steam the hens ahead of time, leaving only the final frying, which takes just a few minutes.
So-called Cornish hens are really just what the French call poussin — immature or spring chickens. They are ideal for this dish, but you can also use regular chicken pieces.
In a perfect world, one's spice cabinet would have all the dry spices called for (as options) in this recipe. Use what you have in whatever combinations that please your palate.

FROM
THE ASIAN BISTRO
COOKBOOK BY
ANDREW CHASE

4	Cornish hens, split in half	4
3 tbsp	soya sauce	45 mL
2 tbsp	Chinese rice wine or sake or dry sherry	25 mL
8	slices ginger root	8
4	green onions, cut into a few pieces each	4
1/2 tsp	black peppercorns or 1/4 tsp (1 mL) ground black pepper	2 mL
12	Chinese dried lily buds (optional)	12
1 cup	cooking oil	250 mL
	Coriander leaves for garnish (optional)	

Optional Spices

1 tsp	Szechuan peppercorns	5 mL
3	split black cardamom pods or 1/4 tsp (1 mL) ground cardamom	3
2	star anise or 1/4 tsp (1 mL) ground fennel or anise seed	2
1	3- inch (8 cm) piece cinnamon bark or 1/4 tsp (1 mL) ground cinnamon	1
6	cloves or 1/4 tsp (1 mL) ground cloves	6
3	slices nutmeg seed or 1/4 tsp (1 mL) ground nutmeg	3
	or	
1 1/2 tsp	5-spice powder (see page 64)	7 mL

1. Mix all the ingredients except the oil and coriander leaves together in a large bowl; marinate 1 to 2 hours at room temperature.

2. Arrange the hens skin-side up in the bowl in a single layer. Put 2 inches (5 cm) water in a covered pot that can hold the bowl. Place a small bowl (such as a rice or cereal bowl, ramekin or low rimmed plate) in the bottom of the pot, putting a little water in it also, and stand the bowl with the cornish hens on it. Bring the water to a boil, lower to a high simmer and cover the pot. (If you have a steamer, simply place the bowl in the steamer over boiling water.) Steam for 25 minutes.

Recipe continues...

Remove the bowl from the steamer. When cool enough to handle, remove hens from bowl; pick off the whole spices. Strain the liquid in the bowl into a small saucepan and cook down by about half or until slightly thickened, skimming any scum off the surface (keep it warm if you are going to finish the hens immediately). The recipe can be prepared ahead of time up to this point.

3. Heat the oil in a skillet and fry the hens, turning once, until the skin is nicely crisped and colored. Reheat the sauce, if necessary, and serve in small sauceplates on the side or in a pool under the cornish hen pieces. Garnish with coriander leaves if desired.

Chicken Baked in Coconut-Lime Cream

Serves 4

I originally devised this recipe for guinea fowl. It is based on a Vietnamese preparation for pigeon, where the coconut cream bastes the lean meat of the bird. It also works beautifully for chicken, especially leaner free-range chickens, and makes for an attractive presentation.
The chicken is first marinated overnight, then baked with a fragrant coconut cream; the result is very rich and moist with a complex flavor. Serve with white rice and a sautéed green vegetable, with cucumber salad on the side to help cut the richness of the coconut cream.
As in other chicken dishes where the fowl is marinated, I prefer air-chilled (not water chilled) poultry. This method of chilling helps retain the flavor and prevents the spread of bacteria (especially salmonella) from bird to bird. Refrigerate unopened cans of coconut milk for an hour to solidify the coconut cream, making it easier to remove.

13- BY 9-INCH (3 L) BAKING DISH

1	chicken (2 to 3 lbs [1 to 1.5 kg]) or 4 chicken breasts (bone-in or boneless, but with skin attached)	1
2	stalks lemon grass, very finely chopped	2
4 tsp	minced ginger root	20 mL
6	cloves, garlic	6
1/2 cup	coarsely chopped onions	125 mL
2 tbsp	lime juice	25 mL
2 tbsp	fish sauce or 6 anchovies mixed with 2 tbsp (25 mL) water	25 mL
1 1/2 tsp	brown sugar	7 mL
1 tsp	black pepper	5 mL
1/2 tsp	ground cumin	2 mL
2	cans (14 oz [400 mL]) coconut milk	2
2	green finger chilies or 6 green bird-eye chilies	2
1	lime, juiced and rind grated	1
2	stalks coriander, stems and leaves, chopped	2
2 tsp	granulated sugar	10 mL
3/4 tsp	salt	4 mL
	Coriander leaves, mint (optional)	
	Lime wedges (optional)	

1. Halve the whole chicken by cutting through the breast bone, opening the chicken up and cutting out the back bone (keep it for stock).

2. In a blender, combine lemon grass, ginger, garlic, onion, lime juice and fish sauce; chop as finely as possible. Mix in the sugar, black pepper and cumin. Rub this mixture all over both sides of the chicken; place skin-side up in a shallow glass dish, cover with plastic wrap and refrigerate overnight or up to 3 days.

3. Bring chicken to room temperature. Preheat oven to

FROM
THE ASIAN BISTRO
COOKBOOK BY
ANDREW CHASE

If you live in a city with a sizeable Thai population, you might be able to find kaffir limes and lime leaves. The small, wrinkly limes are grown for their extremely fragrant peel and leaves. Dried leaves are sold at Asian grocers, but have little of the fragrance of fresh ones. Fresh leaves will keep refrigerated for 5 to 7 days and will freeze very well; they need but a minute to defrost. Note that defrosted leaves will turn brown in the refrigerator after one day, so defrost only what you need. When using the leaves, be sure to pull out the middle vein. In this recipe, the lime peel can be replaced by the grated peel of 1 kaffir lime. For extra fragrance, add 2 or 3 very finely chopped lime leaves. To chop, cut or pull out the veins, then roll 2 or 3 halves up into a small cylinder. With a very sharp knife, cut thread-thin slices across the cylinder then chop the threads finely.

375° F (190° C). Open the cans of coconut milk without shaking or agitating the cans; remove the top half to two-thirds of the coconut milk (you should have about 3 cups [750 mL] of coconut cream). Discard the remaining thin coconut milk or save it for another use. For a mild sauce, seed the chilies and chop very finely; for a spicier version, keep the seeds in and chop as finely as you can, making sure the seeds are chopped up well. Mix the thick coconut cream with the chilies, lime juice and rind, coriander, sugar and salt. Pour over chicken.

4. Bake, uncovered, 30 to 40 minutes for the breasts or 40 to 50 minutes for the half-chickens. Garnish with plenty of coriander leaves, a few sprigs of mint and lime wedges, if desired.

Thyme-Roasted Chicken with Garlic Gravy

Serves 4

I feel like it's a special occasion when I have a roast chicken in the oven. It conjures up a homey smell and feel. In my opinion, it's one of the most satisfying dishes on earth.
Here we place herbs and seasonings under the bird's skin to produce a succulent, flavorful chicken. Slow roasting with lots of garlic creates a wonderful aroma — yet, surprisingly, imparts only a subtle flavor to the gravy.

TIP

In a rush to roast a chicken? Increase oven temperature to 400° F (200° C) and roast bird for about 1 1/4 hours. Make sure to add extra stock to the pan — it evaporates during roasting — and baste bird often.

FROM
THE COMFORT FOOD COOKBOOK BY JOHANNA BURKHARD

PREHEAT OVEN TO 325° F (160° C)
ROASTING PAN WITH RACK

1	chicken (about 3 1/2 lbs [1.75 kg])	1
10	cloves garlic, peeled	10
1 tsp	dried thyme	5 mL
1/4 tsp	salt	1 mL
1/4 tsp	pepper	1 mL
1 1/4 cups	chicken stock	300 mL
1/2 cup	white wine *or* additional chicken stock	125 mL
1 tbsp	all-purpose flour	15 mL

1. Remove giblets and neck from chicken. Rinse and pat dry chicken inside and out. Place 2 cloves garlic inside cavity. Starting at cavity opening, gently lift skin and rub thyme, salt and pepper over breasts and legs. Tie legs together with string; tuck wings under back.

2. Add remaining garlic, half the chicken stock and the wine to roasting pan; place chicken, breast side up, on rack in pan.

3. Roast in preheated oven, basting every 30 minutes, adding additional stock if pan juices evaporate, for 1 3/4 to 2 hours or until pan juices run clear when chicken is pierced and meat thermometer inserted in thigh registers 185° F (85° C).

4. Transfer to a platter; tent with foil and let stand for 10 minutes before carving. Meanwhile, strain pan juices into measure, pressing down firmly to mash garlic into juices; skim off fat. Add enough of remaining stock to make 3/4 cup (175 mL).

5. In a small saucepan, stir together 2 tbsp (25 mL) of pan juices and flour; cook, stirring, over medium heat for 1 minute. Gradually whisk in remaining pan juices; cook, stirring, until boiling and thickened. Serve with chicken.

Chicken-Vegetable Cobbler

Serves 6

Some dishes never lose their appeal — like this old-fashioned favorite, which is perfect to make on a lazy Sunday afternoon. It requires a little time to prepare, but once the creamy chicken mixture and its golden biscuit crust is bubbling away in the oven, you'll be glad you made the effort. And so will your family.

TIP

I've chosen a biscuit crust to make this a cobbler, but you can cover the savory chicken filling with your favorite pie pastry or frozen puff pastry to make a pot pie.

•

Or you can omit the topping altogether and serve over rice or noodles.

•

The chicken-vegetable mixture without the crust freezes well for up to 3 months.

•

Fine herbs, available in the spice section of your grocery store, contains dried parsley, chives, tarragon and chervil. You can also use an Italian herb mix of basil, oregano and marjoram.

PREHEAT OVEN TO 400° F (200° C)
12-CUP (3 L) DEEP CASSEROLE DISH

2 lbs	chicken legs, with thighs, skin and excess fat removed	1 kg
3 1/2 cups	water	875 mL
1 tsp	salt	5 mL
	Pepper to taste	
1	bay leaf	1
2 tbsp	butter	25 mL
2 cups	quartered mushrooms	500 mL
1	medium onion, chopped	1
1	large garlic clove, minced	1
2 tsp	dried fine herbs or dried basil	10 mL
1/3 cup	all-purpose flour	75 mL
3	carrots, peeled and sliced	3
2	stalks celery, chopped	2
1/2 cup	whipping (35%) cream or light (15%) cream	125 mL
1 cup	frozen peas	250 mL
1/4 cup	chopped fresh parsley	50 mL
	Salt and pepper to taste	
	Cheddar Biscuit Crust (recipe follows)	

1. In a large saucepan, combine chicken, water, salt, pepper and bay leaf. Bring to a boil; reduce heat to medium-low, cover and simmer for 1 hour. Let stand until chicken is cool enough to handle. Pull chicken meat from bones; cut into bite-sized pieces. Strain stock, skim off any fat; there should be 2 1/2 cups (625 mL) of stock. Add water, if necessary. Discard bay leaf.

2. In large saucepan, melt butter over medium heat; cook mushrooms, onions, garlic and fine herbs, stirring often, for 5 minutes or until softened.

3. Blend flour with small amount of stock until smooth; add rest of stock. Stir into mushroom mixture; bring to a boil, stirring, until thickened and smooth.

FROM
THE COMFORT FOOD
COOKBOOK BY
JOHANNA BURKHARD

4. Add carrots and celery; cover and simmer over low heat, stirring occasionally, for 15 minutes or until vegetables are just tender.

5. Add chicken, cream, peas and parsley; season with salt and pepper to taste. Heat through. Spoon hot chicken mixture into casserole dish.

6. Meanwhile make biscuit crust (see below). Roll out on lightly floured board to make a circle large enough to cover casserole. Arrange on top of hot chicken mixture. (If making chicken mixture ahead, cover and refrigerate; microwave at Medium-High, or reheat in saucepan on stovetop until piping hot before topping with crust.)

7. Bake in preheated oven for about 25 to 30 minutes or until crust is golden and filling is bubbly.

Cheddar Biscuit Crust

1 1/3 cups	all-purpose flour	325 mL
2 tsp	baking powder	10 mL
1/2 tsp	baking soda	2 mL
1/4 tsp	salt	1 mL
1/2 cup	shredded Cheddar cheese (optional)	125 mL
1/2 cup	buttermilk	125 mL
1/4 cup	butter, melted	50 mL

1. In a bowl combine flour, baking powder, baking soda and salt. Add cheese, if using. Combine buttermilk and butter; stir into flour mixture to make a soft dough.

Rosemary Chicken Breasts with Layered Potatoes and Onions

A breeze to prepare, this easy-to-assemble dish is elegant enough to serve to company. The herb and lemon butter tucked under the skins keeps the chicken moist and I love the way it imparts a wonderful flavor to the vegetables layered on the bottom.

TIP

Make extra batches of rosemary butter, shape into small logs, wrap in plastic and store in the freezer.
Cut into slices and use to tuck under the breast skins of whole roasting chickens or Cornish hens, or to top grilled meats.

FROM
THE COMFORT FOOD
COOKBOOK BY
JOHANNA BURKHARD

PREHEAT OVEN TO 375° F (190° C)
13- BY 9-INCH (3 L) SHALLOW BAKING DISH, OILED

3	medium potatoes (about 1 lb [500 g])	3
2	small sweet potatoes (about 1 lb [500 g])	2
1	medium onion	1
1 tsp	dried rosemary, crumbled	5 mL
	Salt and pepper to taste	
4	single chicken breasts with skin	4

Rosemary Butter

2 tbsp	butter	25 mL
1	large clove garlic, minced	1
1 tsp	grated lemon rind	5 mL
1 tsp	dried rosemary, crumbled	5 mL
1/4 tsp	salt	1 mL
1/4 tsp	pepper	1 mL

1. Peel potatoes, sweet potatoes and onion; cut into very thin slices. Layer vegetables in prepared baking dish. Season with rosemary, salt and pepper.

2. Place whole chicken breasts, skin side up, on work surface. (If you purchased whole breasts with backs on, cut away back bone using poultry shears.) Remove any fat deposits under skins. Press down on breast bone to flatten slightly.

3. Make the rosemary butter: In a small bowl, mash together butter, garlic, lemon rind, rosemary, salt and pepper. Divide into 4 portions.

4. Carefully loosen the breast skins and tuck rosemary butter under skins, patting to distribute evenly.

5. Arrange chicken on top of vegetables in baking dish. Cover with sheet of greased foil; roast in preheated oven for 45 minutes. Uncover and roast 25 to 30 minutes more or until vegetables are tender and chicken is nicely colored.

5-Spice Chicken with Ginger and Scallion Lo Mein

Serves 4

This is basically a roasted version of the poached soya chicken so popular in Chinese noodle shops. Roasting gives the chicken a more concentrated flavor. It's delicious with ginger and scallions.

FROM
NEW WORLD NOODLES BY BILL JONES & STEPHEN WONG

PREHEAT OVEN TO 375° F (190° C)

1/2 tsp	HOME-STYLE 5-SPICE MIX (see recipe, page 64) *or* commercially prepared 5-spice powder	2 mL
1/2 tsp	freshly ground black pepper	2 mL
1 tbsp	coarsely chopped garlic	15 mL
1 tbsp	brown sugar	15 mL
1 tbsp	dark soya sauce *or* mushroom soya sauce	15 mL
1 tbsp	fish sauce	15 mL
1 tsp	sesame oil	5 mL
2	large chicken breasts	2
1	recipe GINGER AND SCALLION LO MEIN (see page 64)	1

1. In a small bowl, combine 5-spice, pepper, garlic, sugar, soya sauce, fish sauce and sesame oil; mix well. Rub marinade evenly over chicken; cover and refrigerate for 4 hours or overnight, turning occasionally.

2. Place chicken in roasting pan and pour any residual marinade over the chicken. Roast for 20 minutes, then baste with pan drippings. Continue cooking for an additional 10 minutes or until liquid runs clear when the thickest part of the breast is pierced with a fork. If necessary, turn the broiler on and brown the chicken on each side until it is crisp (being careful not to burn, which happens quickly) about 1 minute per side.

3. Meanwhile, prepare Ginger Scallion Lo Mein up to the point of cooking the noodles. Keep a pot of boiling water ready for the noodles.

4. Remove chicken from oven. Allow to rest for 2 minutes, then divide into 4 portions. Complete Ginger Scallion Lo Mein and serve as an accompaniment.

Home-Style 5-Spice Mix

2 tbsp	fennel seeds	25 mL
2 tbsp	clove sticks	25 mL
2 tbsp	star anise	25 mL
2 tbsp	Szechuan peppercorns	25 mL
2	cinnamon sticks (or 2 tsp [10 mL] ground cinnamon)	2

1. In a nonstick pan over medium-high heat, cook the spices, shaking the pan constantly. When the pan just begins to smoke, remove from the heat. Transfer contents to a plate to cool.

2. In a small coffee or spice grinder (you can also use a mortar and pestle, blender or food processor) grind spices until a fine powder is obtained. Transfer to a small, sealable plastic container and reserve until needed.

Ginger and Scallion Lo Mein

Serves 4 to 6

as a side dish

Lo Mein describes a technique that generally involves mixing a flavoring sauce with blanched noodles, requiring no further cooking. This classic Chinese noodle shop dish is often served with a small bowl of broth on the side, in case the noodles are too dry.

1 tbsp	vegetable oil, plus oil for coating noodles	15 mL
1/2 cup	finely chopped green onions	125 mL
2 tbsp	minced ginger root	25 mL
2 tbsp	chicken stock	25 mL
1/2 tsp	salt, or to taste	2 mL
1 lb	fresh wunton noodles or 8 oz (250 g) dried thin egg noodles	500 g

1. In a nonstick wok or skillet, heat oil over medium heat for 30 seconds. Add ginger root and green onions and stir-fry for 30 seconds. Add chicken stock and salt; cook for 1 minute. Remove from heat.

2. In a large pot of boiling salted water, cook noodles until al dente, about 2 minutes. (If using dried noodles, prepare according to package directions.) Drain.

3. Immediately transfer noodles to a serving bowl, add sauce and toss to mix. Serve hot as an accompaniment.

Chinese Chicken with Garlic Ginger Sauce

Serves 6

TIP

This is delicious served cold.

•

This is a simple-looking chicken dish, but unbelievably tasty. Great for leftovers. Increase garlic and ginger to taste

MAKE AHEAD

Prepare up to a day ahead and serve at room temperature.

FROM
ROSE REISMAN'S
ENLIGHTENED HOME COOKING

3 lb	whole chicken	1.5 kg
Sauce		
1/3 cup	chicken stock	75 mL
1/4 cup	chopped green onions (about 2 medium)	50 mL
3 tbsp	vegetable oil	45 mL
4 tsp	soya sauce	20 mL
1 tsp	minced garlic	5 mL
1 tsp	minced ginger root	5 mL

1. Remove neck and giblets from chicken and discard. Place chicken in large saucepan and add water to cover. Cover saucepan and bring to a boil over high heat. Reduce heat to low and simmer, covered, for 45 minutes, or until juices run clear from chicken leg when pierced.

2. Meanwhile, whisk together stock, green onions, oil, soya sauce, garlic and ginger in a small bowl.

3. Remove chicken from pot and let cool slightly. Remove skin; cut into serving pieces. Serve with dipping sauce.

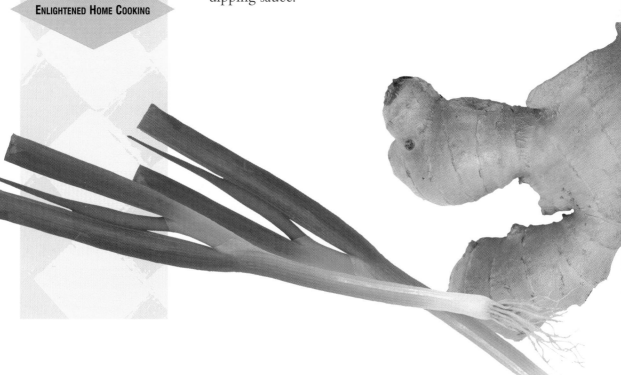

Tagine Chicken with Lemon, Olives and Grapes

Serves 2 or 3

The tagine is a two-piece earthenware contraption with which the Moroccans perform the most saucy of culinary magic. Coals glow and spread warmth to the clay pot on the top half of the tagine, peppering with smoke the already-spicy-earthy sauces that simmer within. The concoctions always include meat, a vegetable and plenty of sauce — ideal for sopping up with dark, chewy bread (the sole accompaniment to tagine). The lightest and most heart-warming tagine of all is chicken, cooked here with lemon, olives and grapes. I offer a version that uses only skinless breast meat and cooks up in 15 minutes total time, instead of the original version for whole chicken that takes an hour and a half. I also suggest a nonstick frying pan, because I doubt many of us could get away with a coal-burning cooking device in the apartment.

FROM
SIMPLY
MEDITERRANEAN COOKING
BY BYRON AYANOGLU &
ALGIS KEMEZYS

8 oz	skinless boneless chicken breast, cut into 1/2-inch (1 cm) strips	250 g
2 tbsp	all-purpose flour	25 mL
2 tbsp	olive oil	25 mL
1/2 tsp	ground coriander	2 mL
1/2 tsp	ground cumin	2 mL
1/4 tsp	salt	1 mL
1/4 tsp	freshly ground black pepper	1 mL
1 cup	finely diced onions	250 mL
2	pinches saffron threads or 1 pinch turmeric	2
1 tbsp	lemon juice	15 mL
6	thin (1/8-inch [3 mm]) cross-section wheels of lemon, with peel, seeded	6
6	black olives, pitted and halved	6
1/2 cup	frozen peas	125 mL
1 cup	chicken stock	250 mL
16	green seedless grapes	16
	Steamed rice or couscous as an accompaniment	
	Few sprigs fresh coriander or parsley, chopped	

1. Lightly dredge chicken in flour and set aside.

2. In a large nonstick frying pan, heat oil, coriander, cumin, salt and pepper over high heat for 30 seconds. Add chicken and onions in a single layer; sprinkle chicken as evenly as possible with saffron threads. Stir-fry for 2 minutes or until chicken is lightly browned and onions are softened.

3. Add lemon juice; cook, stirring, 30 seconds or until sizzling. Immediately add lemon slices, olives and frozen peas; fold once or twice to mix. Add chicken stock and bring to a boil, stirring. Reduce heat to medium-low and cook, stirring lightly, for about 4 minutes or until the sauce is shiny and syrupy. Stir in grapes; cook for 1 more minute. Remove from heat.

4. Portion alongside plain steamed rice or couscous with plenty of sauce. Garnish with chopped fresh coriander and serve immediately.

Chicken Fournisto with Vegetables

Serves 4

"Fournisto" is the Greek term for "cooked in the oven" — which may not sound terribly exotic to North American ears, but growing up in Istanbul (where few homes were equipped with ovens), it signified something special. Every Sunday, the ready-to-bake dish would have to be taken to the local bakery where, for a fee, it would be baked in the late morning (after all the bread was done), then fetched when ready. Not surprisingly, when we moved to Canada and discovered an oven in our apartment, my mother took full advantage of this luxury, feeding me "fournisto" chicken almost daily. Here I expand on her original recipe with some additional vegetables and a shorter bake in a hotter oven. This one-pot meal is easy to serve; if need be, it can be baked, taken out of the oven to wait and then gently reheated (in a 250° F [120° C] oven for 15 minutes) without any loss in quality.

LARGE ROASTING PAN WITH LID
PREHEAT OVEN TO 425° F (220° C)

4	medium potatoes (about 1 lb [500 g])	4
1	yam or sweet potato, scrubbed	1
1 tbsp	vegetable oil	15 mL
4	chicken legs with thighs attached (2 1/2 to 3 lbs [1.25 to 1.5 kg])	4
1	medium onion, peeled and quartered	1
4	cloves garlic, peeled	4
1	green pepper, trimmed and quartered	1
6	plum tomatoes, quartered	6
1 cup	boiling chicken stock	250 mL
2 tbsp	lemon juice	25 mL
1 tbsp	sweet paprika	15 mL
1 tsp	dried oregano	5 mL
1 tsp	granulated sugar	5 mL
1/2 tsp	salt	2 mL
1/4 tsp	freshly ground black pepper	1 mL
	Few sprigs fresh parsley, chopped	

1. Bring a pot of water to a boil. Add whole potatoes and yam; reduce heat to medium and cook for 7 minutes or until barely pierceable. Drain, cut into quarters and set aside.

2. Spread oil over bottom of roasting pan. Add chicken legs, potatoes and yams, more-or-less in a single layer (a little overlapping is fine). Fit onion, garlic and green pepper in empty spots. Distribute tomatoes over everything.

3. Stir together boiling chicken stock, lemon juice, paprika, oregano, sugar, salt and pepper. Pour one-half of

FROM
SIMPLY
MEDITERRANEAN COOKING
BY BYRON AYANOGLU &
ALGIS KEMEZYS

mixture evenly over the chicken and vegetables (reserve the rest of the stock). Cover roasting pan. Bake undisturbed for 30 minutes.

4. Remove pan from oven. Toss and turn vegetables and baste chicken with the juices. Return to oven and bake, uncovered, for 15 minutes. Remove from oven and reduce oven temperature to 350° F (180° C). Bring the remaining stock to a boil; pour over chicken and stir in. Return to the oven and let bake, uncovered, for 30 to 45 minutes or until the sauce is reduced and the chicken is falling off the bone. Remove from oven and let rest, covered, for 5 to 10 minutes. Garnish with parsley and serve.

Chicken and Eggplant Parmesan

FROM
ROSE REISMAN'S
ENLIGHTENED HOME
COOKING

Serves 4

TIP

Turkey, veal or pork scallopini can replace chicken.

A stronger cheese, such as Swiss, can replace mozzarella.

A great dish to reheat the next day.

MAKE AHEAD

Prepare earlier in the day, refrigerate and bake at 350° F (180° C) until warm (approximately 10 minutes).

PREHEAT OVEN TO 425° F (220° C)
BAKING SHEET SPRAYED WITH VEGETABLE SPRAY

4	crosswise slices of eggplant, skin on, approximately 1/2 inch (1 cm) thick	4
1	whole egg	1
1	egg white	1
1 tbsp	water or milk	15 mL
2/3 cup	seasoned bread crumbs	150 mL
3 tbsp	chopped fresh parsley (or 2 tsp [10 mL] dried)	45 mL
1 tbsp	grated Parmesan cheese	15 mL
1 lb	skinless boneless chicken breasts (about 4)	500 g
2 tsp	vegetable oil	10 mL
1 tsp	minced garlic	5 mL
1/2 cup	tomato pasta sauce	125 mL
1/2 cup	grated mozzarella cheese	125 mL

1. In small bowl, whisk together whole egg, egg white and water. On plate stir together bread crumbs, parsley and Parmesan. Dip eggplant slices in egg wash, then coat with bread-crumb mixture. Place on prepared pan and bake for 20 minutes, or until tender, turning once.

2. Meanwhile, pound chicken breasts between sheets of waxed paper to 1/4-inch (5 mm) thickness. Dip chicken in remaining egg wash, then coat with remaining bread-crumb mixture. Heat oil and garlic in nonstick skillet sprayed with vegetable spray and cook for 4 minutes, or until golden brown, turning once.

3. Spread 1 tbsp (15 mL) of tomato sauce on each eggplant slice. Place one chicken breast on top of each eggplant slice. Spread another 1 tbsp (15 mL) of tomato sauce on top of each chicken piece. Sprinkle with cheese and bake for 5 minutes or until cheese melts.

Rock Salt Pan-Roasted Chicken in Garlic Sesame and Olive Oil

Serves 4

Perhaps because chicken was first domesticated in China and later exported to all corners of the world, the Chinese have a special affinity for dishes featuring crispy roasted poultry. In this recipe, seasoning the bird with coarse salt and roasting to a golden brown brings out the flavor of the chicken and produces a delicious crispy skin. Simple and elegant, hot or cold, this is true comfort food.

FROM
NEW WORLD CHINESE COOKING BY BILL JONES & STEPHEN WONG

PREHEAT OVEN TO 375° F (190° C)
10-INCH (25 CM) OVENPROOF FRYING PAN OR CAST IRON SKILLET OR 9- BY 13-INCH (3 L) BAKING DISH

2 tbsp	olive oil	25 mL
1	onion, thinly sliced	1
1	head garlic, separated into cloves, peeled	1
3 lbs	chicken pieces	1.5 Kg
2 tbsp	coarse salt (sea salt or pickling salt)	25 mL
1 tsp	sesame oil	5 mL
	Cracked black pepper to taste	
	GINGER GREEN ONION PESTO, optional (see recipe, page 74)	

1. In a skillet, preferably ovenproof, heat oil over high heat for 30 seconds. Add onions and garlic; sauté 2 minutes. (If you don't have an ovenproof skillet, transfer sautéed garlic and onions to baking dish and proceed as follows.)

2. Arrange chicken pieces on top of onion mixture; sprinkle evenly with salt and drizzle with sesame oil. Place the skillet or baking dish in preheated oven and roast for 45 minutes or until the skin is golden brown. Remove from oven; allow to rest 2 to 3 minutes.

3. Transfer to a platter and serve with steamed rice and Ginger Green Onion Pesto, if desired.

Ginger Green Onion Pesto

Makes 2 1/2 cups (625 mL)

This pesto is a simple mixture of green onions laced with ginger and melded together by sesame seeds. It's excellent on chicken and makes a great addition to soups and salads or served over plain rice.

•

The pesto keeps 1 week in the refrigerator.

1 cup	sliced green onions	250 mL
2 tbsp	minced ginger root	25 mL
1 tsp	salt	5 mL
1 cup	vegetable oil	250 mL
1/2 cup	sesame seeds	125 mL

1. In a food processor or blender, combine all ingredients. Pulse on and off until the mixture achieves a uniform consistency. Transfer to a sealable container and refrigerate.

Pasta

Chicken Stir-Fry with Asparagus, Bok Choy and Oyster Sauce

12 oz	skinless boneless chicken breast, cut into thin strips	375 g
2 tsp	vegetable oil	10 mL
2 cups	asparagus cut into 1-inch (2.5 cm) pieces	500 mL
1 cup	sliced red peppers	250 mL
4 cups	sliced bok choy or napa cabbage	1 L
1 cup	water chestnuts	250 mL

Sauce

3/4 cup	chicken stock	175 mL
3 tbsp	oyster sauce	45 mL
1 1/2 tbsp	rice wine vinegar	22 mL
2 tbsp	honey	25 mL
1 tbsp	soya sauce	15 mL
1 tbsp	cornstarch	15 mL
1 1/2 tsp	minced garlic	7 mL
1 1/2 tsp	minced ginger root	7 mL
1/2 cup	chopped green onions (about 4 medium)	125 mL

1. Sauce: In bowl, whisk together stock, oyster sauce, vinegar, honey, soya sauce, cornstarch, garlic and ginger; set aside.

2. In a nonstick skillet or wok sprayed with vegetable spray, stir-fry chicken strips for 3 to 4 minutes, stirring constantly, or until just cooked at center. Remove chicken from skillet.

3. Heat oil in skillet over high heat. Add asparagus and red pepper strips and stir-fry for 3 minutes, stirring constantly, or until tender-crisp. Add bok choy and water chestnuts and stir-fry for 1 minute or until bok choy wilts. Stir sauce again and add to wok along with chicken strips. Cook for 2 minutes or until thickened slightly. Garnish with green onions.

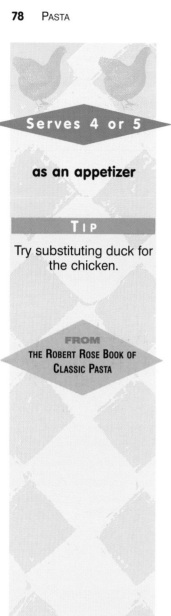

Serves 4 or 5

as an appetizer

TIP

Try substituting duck for
the chicken.

FROM
THE ROBERT ROSE BOOK OF
CLASSIC PASTA

Penne with Mushrooms and Chicken

2 tbsp	butter	25 mL
2 tbsp	olive oil	25 mL
2	cloves garlic, crushed	2
1 cup	chopped onions	250 mL
1 tbsp	chopped fresh basil (or 1/2 tsp [2 mL] dried)	15 mL
1 tbsp	chopped fresh parsley (or 1 tsp [5 mL] dried)	15 mL
1/4 cup	white wine	50 mL
1/4 cup	chicken stock	50 mL
1/2 cup	whipping (35%) cream	125 mL
8 oz	penne	250 g
2 tbsp	butter	25 mL
2 tbsp	olive oil	25 mL
4 oz	cooked chicken (preferably smoked), sliced	125 g
4 oz	mushrooms (preferably a variety), chopped	125 g
1	tomato, chopped	1
1	small bunch arugula, chopped	1
1/3 cup	grated Parmesan cheese	75 mL

1. In a large skillet, heat butter and oil over medium heat. Add garlic, onion, basil and parsley; cook until onions are softened. Stir in wine; cook 2 minutes. Stir in chicken stock; cook 2 minutes. Stir in cream; cook 5 minutes. Set sauce aside.

2. In a large pot of boiling water, cook penne 8 to 10 minutes or until al dente. Meanwhile, prepare the sauce.

3. In another large skillet, heat butter and oil over medium heat. Cook chicken, mushrooms, tomato and arugula 3 minutes. Stir in cream sauce; reduce heat to low and cook 5 minutes.

4. Toss drained pasta with sauce. Serve immediately, sprinkled with Parmesan.

Rotini with Chicken, Sweet Peppers and Sun-Dried Tomato Sauce

12 oz	rotini	375 g
12 oz	skinless, boneless chicken breasts cut into 1-inch (2.5 cm) strips	375 g
1 1/2 cups	thinly sliced yellow or green sweet peppers	375 mL
1/4 cup	grated Asiago or Romano cheese	50 mL

Sauce

4 oz	sun-dried tomatoes	100 g
2 tsp	crushed garlic	10 mL
1 cup	chicken stock or water	250 mL
1/2 cup	chopped parsley	125 mL
2 tbsp	toasted pine nuts	25 mL
3 tbsp	olive oil	45 mL
3 tbsp	grated Parmesan cheese	45 mL

1. Cover sun-dried tomatoes with boiling water; let soak for 15 minutes. Drain and chop. Set aside.

2. Cook pasta in boiling water according to package instructions or until firm to the bite. Drain and place in serving bowl.

3. In large nonstick skillet sprayed with nonstick vegetable spray, sauté chicken until no longer pink, approximately 5 minutes. Add to pasta.

4. Respray skillet and sauté sweet peppers just until tender, approximately 4 minutes. Add to pasta with Asiago cheese.

5. Make the sauce: In food processor, combine sun-dried tomatoes, garlic, stock, parsley, nuts, oil and cheese. Purée until smooth. Pour over pasta, and toss.

Shanghai Noodles with Shredded Chicken, Chinese Cabbage and a Spicy Sesame Sauce

Serves 4

A traditional version of this dish would consist of shredded beef and Chinese cabbage tossed with soya sauce. For a change of pace we've used chicken breast and spiced up the sauce with chili paste and sesame seeds.

•

Shred cabbage by cutting into thin strips, starting at the tip of the leaves.

•

If using a green cabbage cut the head in quarters, remove core and shred.

FROM
New World Noodles by Bill Jones & Stephen Wong

1 lb	fresh Shanghai noodles *or* 8 oz (250 g) dried spaghetti	500 g
1 tbsp	vegetable oil, plus oil for coating noodles	15 mL
8 oz	boneless skinless chicken breast	250 g
2 tbsp	cornstarch	25 mL
3 cups	shredded Chinese cabbage *or* green cabbage	750 mL
1 tsp	minced ginger root	5 mL
1 tsp	minced garlic	5 mL
2 tbsp	water	25 mL
1 tbsp	dark soya sauce	15 mL
1 tbsp	chopped cilantro	15 mL
1 tsp	chili paste (or to taste)	5 mL
1 tsp	sesame oil	5 mL
1 tbsp	toasted sesame seeds, plus extra seeds for garnish	15 mL
	Sliced green onion for garnish	

1. In a heatproof bowl or pot, cover noodles with boiling water and soak for 5 minutes. (If using pasta, prepare according to package directions.) Drain, toss with a little oil and set aside.

2. On a cutting board, cut chicken into thin slices and then cut each slice into thin strips. Dredge strips in cornstarch, shaking off excess starch. Set aside.

3. In a nonstick wok or skillet, heat oil over medium-high heat for 30 seconds. Add ginger root and cook until it starts to sizzle. Add chicken and sauté until brown, about 4 to 5 minutes. Add cabbage and garlic and stir-fry until cabbage is wilted. Add water. Cook, covered, over low heat for 2 minutes.

4. Add soya sauce, cilantro, chili paste, sesame oil and sesame seeds to the mixture; toss well. Garnish with green onions and additional sesame seeds, if desired. Serve immediately.

Chicken and Tarragon Pasta Pizza

PREHEAT OVEN TO 350°F (180°C)
10-INCH (3 L) SPRINGFORM PAN SPRAYED
WITH VEGETABLE SPRAY

6 oz	broken fettuccine	150 g
1	egg	1
1/3 cup	2% milk	75 mL
3 tbsp	grated Parmesan cheese	45 mL
1 cup	chopped broccoli	250 mL
1 1/2 tsp	crushed garlic	7 mL
8 oz	skinless, boneless chicken breasts, cut into 1-inch (2.5-cm) cubes	250 g
2/3 cup	diced sweet green peppers	150 mL
2/3 cup	diced red onions	150 mL
1 cup	cold chicken stock	250 mL
1 cup	2% milk	250 mL
3 tbsp	all-purpose flour	45 mL
1/4 cup	chopped fresh tarragon (or 3 tsp [15 mL] dried)	50 mL
2 1/2 oz	shredded Swiss or mozzarella cheese	60 g

1. Cook pasta in boiling water according to package instructions or until firm to the bite. Drain and place in mixing bowl. Add egg, milk and cheese; mix well and pour in pan. Bake for 20 minutes.

2. Blanch broccoli in boiling water just until tender. Drain, rinse with cold water, and set aside.

3. In large nonstick skillet sprayed with vegetable spray, sauté garlic and chicken until chicken is no longer pink, approximately 4 minutes. Set chicken aside.

4. Spray skillet again with vegetable spray; sauté green peppers and onions for 4 minutes. In small bowl, mix stock, milk and flour until smooth. Add to skillet with broccoli, chicken and tarragon. Simmer on low heat until sauce thickens, approximately 4 minutes, stirring constantly. Pour into pan, sprinkle with cheese. Bake for 10 minutes.

Chicken Cacciatore over Penne

12 oz	penne	375 g
2 tsp	vegetable oil	10 mL
2 tsp	crushed garlic	10 mL
1 1/3 cups	chopped onions	325 mL
1 1/4 cups	chopped sweet red peppers	300 mL
1 1/2 cups	sliced mushrooms	375 mL
1 lb	skinless, boneless chicken breasts, cubed	500 g
1/2 cup	dry red wine	125 mL
1/3 cup	chicken stock	75 mL
2 3/4 cups	fresh or canned tomatoes, crushed	675 mL
1 tbsp	tomato paste	15 mL
2 tsp	dried basil	10 mL
1 tsp	dried oregano	5 mL
1/4 cup	chopped parsley	50 mL

1. Cook pasta in boiling water according to package instructions or until firm to the bite. Drain and place in serving bowl.

2. In large nonstick skillet, heat oil; sauté garlic, onions and red peppers until soft, approximately 5 minutes. Add mushrooms and sauté until soft, approximately 5 minutes. Add chicken and sauté on medium heat until just no longer pink, approximately 5 minutes.

3. Add wine and stock; simmer for 2 minutes. Add tomatoes, tomato paste, basil and oregano; simmer for 15 minutes, covered, on low heat, stirring occasionally. Pour over pasta. Add parsley, and toss.

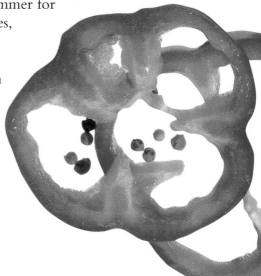

Linguine with Pesto Chicken

12 oz	linguine	375 g
12 oz	skinless, boneless chicken breasts, thinly sliced	375 g

Sauce

2 cups	fresh basil, packed down	500 mL
1/3 cup	chicken stock	75 mL
3 tbsp	olive oil	45 mL
2 tbsp	grated Parmesan cheese	25 mL
2 tbsp	toasted pine nuts or walnuts	25 mL
1 1/2 tsp	crushed garlic	7 mL

1. Cook pasta in boiling water according to package instructions or until firm to the bite. Drain and place in serving bowl.

2. In medium nonstick skillet sprayed with vegetable spray, sauté chicken until no longer pink, approximately 3 minutes. Add to pasta.

3. Make the sauce: In food processor, purée basil, stock, oil, cheese, nuts and garlic until smooth. Pour over pasta, and toss.

Serves 6 to 8

TIP

Replace chicken with beef, veal or pork for a change.

Pineapple juice from frozen concentrate or the juice from canned pineapple can be used.

MAKE AHEAD

Meatballs and sauce can be cooked up to 2 days before. Reheat gently before pouring over pasta.

FROM
ROSE REISMAN BRINGS HOME LIGHT PASTA

Sweet-and-Sour Oriental °
Chickenballs over Spaghetti

10 oz	spaghetti	300 g
12 oz	ground chicken	375 g
1 tsp	crushed garlic	5 mL
1 tsp	minced ginger root	5 mL
3 tbsp	finely chopped onions	45 mL
3 tbsp	canned or home-made tomato sauce	45 mL
1	egg	1
3 tbsp	seasoned bread crumbs	45 mL

Sauce

1 cup	ketchup	250 mL
1 1/2 cups	pineapple juice	375 mL
2 tbsp	brown sugar	25 mL
1 cup	thinly sliced carrots	250 mL
1 cup	thinly sliced red peppers	250 mL
1 cup	pineapple chunks	250 mL

1. Cook pasta in boiling water according to package instructions or until firm to the bite. Drain and place in serving bowl.

2. In bowl, mix together chicken, garlic, ginger, onions, tomato sauce, egg and bread crumbs until well combined. Form into small balls of approximately 1 inch (2.5 cm). This will make about 32 balls.

3. Make the sauce: In large nonstick saucepan, combine ketchup, pineapple juice, brown sugar and carrots over medium heat. Add chicken balls. Cover and simmer for 30 to 40 minutes, just until chicken balls are tender.

4. In the last 10 minutes of cooking, add red peppers and pineapple chunks. Pour over pasta, and toss.

Macaroni with Chicken and Sun-Dried Tomatoes

Serves 6

TIP

Use dry sun-dried tomatoes instead of those in oil.

•

Smoked chicken or turkey, which you can find in specialty markets, gives this dish an intense flavor.

MAKE AHEAD

Prepare sauce early in day. Reheat gently, adding more stock if sauce thickens. Do not overcook chicken.

FROM
ROSE REISMAN BRINGS
HOME LIGHT PASTA

| 1/2 cup | sun-dried tomatoes | 125 mL |
| 12 oz | macaroni | 375 g |

Sauce

2 tsp	margarine *or* butter	10 mL
1 1/2 tsp	crushed garlic	7 mL
2	large green onions, chopped	2
1 1/2 cups	chicken stock	375 mL
3/4 cup	2% milk	175 mL
2 tbsp	all-purpose flour	25 mL
1 1/2 cups	cooked or smoked chicken, diced	375 mL
1/4 cup	grated Parmesan cheese	50 mL

1. Pour boiling water over sun-dried tomatoes, and let soak for 15 minutes. Drain and chop. Set aside.

2. Cook pasta in boiling water according to package instructions or until firm to the bite. Drain and place in serving bowl.

3. Make the sauce: In large nonstick skillet, heat margarine; sauté garlic, onions and sun-dried tomatoes for 2 minutes. Add stock and simmer for 2 minutes.

4. Meanwhile, combine milk and flour in small bowl; slowly add to stock mixture and cook just until slightly thickened, approximately 3 minutes, stirring constantly. Add chicken and cook for 2 more minutes. Toss with pasta. Sprinkle with cheese.

Linguine with Lychees, Chicken and Cashews

Serves 4 to 6

TIP

Lychees are a Chinese fruit available in cans in the Chinese section of the supermarket.

FROM
THE ROBERT ROSE BOOK OF CLASSIC PASTA

1 lb	linguine	500 g
2 tbsp	butter	25 mL
8 oz	cooked chicken, diced (preferably smoked or roasted)	250 g
1	can (4 oz [125 mL]) lychees, drained and chopped	1
1 cup	whipping (35%) cream	250 mL
1 cup	prepared tomato sauce	250 mL
1/3 cup	chopped cashews	75 mL
1/3 cup	chopped green onions	75 mL
1/4 cup	grated Parmesan cheese	50 mL
	Pepper to taste	

1. In a large pot of boiling salted water, cook linguine 8 to 10 minutes or until al dente. Meanwhile, prepare the sauce.

2. In a large skillet, melt butter over medium-high heat. Add chicken and lychees; cook until chicken starts to brown, about 4 minutes. Stir in cream and tomato sauce; cook 5 minutes.

3. Toss drained pasta with sauce, cashews and green onions. Serve immediately, sprinkled with Parmesan and pepper.

Teriyaki Chicken Stir-Fry with Asparagus and Red Peppers

Serves 6

TIP

Replace asparagus with broccoli, snow peas or sugar snap peas. Chicken can be replaced with pork, beef steak or seafood.

MAKE AHEAD

Prepare sauce up to a day ahead. Stir before using.

FROM
ROSE REISMAN'S
ENLIGHTENED HOME
COOKING

Sauce

1/2 cup	chicken stock or water	125 mL
1/4 cup	rice wine vinegar	50 mL
4 tbsp	honey	60 mL
3 tbsp	soya sauce	45 mL
1 tbsp	sesame oil	15 mL
2 tsp	minced garlic	10 mL
2 tsp	minced ginger	10 mL
2 1/2 tsp	cornstarch	12 mL
12 oz	penne	375 g
12 oz	boneless skinless chicken breast, cut into thin strips	375 g
2 tsp	vegetable oil	10 mL
1 1/2 cups	sliced red peppers	375 mL
1 1/2 cups	asparagus cut into 1-inch (2.5 cm) pieces	375 mL

1. In a small bowl, combine stock, vinegar, honey, soya sauce, sesame oil, garlic, ginger and cornstarch; mix well.

2. In large pot of boiling water, cook penne until tender but firm. Drain and place in serving bowl. Meanwhile, in wok or skillet sprayed with vegetable spray, stir-fry chicken for 2 1/2 minutes or until just cooked at center. Drain any excess liquid and remove chicken from wok.

3. Add oil to wok and stir-fry red peppers and asparagus for 4 minutes or until tender-crisp; stir sauce again and add to wok along with chicken. Cook for 1 minute or until slightly thickened. Toss with drained pasta.

Spaghetti with Chicken and Broccoli

1	bunch broccoli, divided into florets	1
4 tsp	olive oil	20 mL
12 oz	chicken breast, diced	375 g
2	plum tomatoes, diced	2
2 tsp	minced garlic	10 mL
2/3 cup	chicken stock	150 mL
12 oz	spaghetti	375 g
1 tbsp	butter	15 mL
	Salt and pepper to taste	

1. In a large pot of boiling water, blanch broccoli for 2 minutes; refresh under cold water and drain. Set aside.

2. In a large skillet, heat oil over medium-high heat. Add chicken, tomatoes, garlic and broccoli; sauté until chicken is barely cooked, about 5 to 8 minutes. Stir in chicken stock and cook until sauce thickens, about 3 minutes.

3. Meanwhile, in a large pot of boiling salted water, cook spaghetti 8 to 10 minutes or until al dente; drain.

4. Toss pasta with sauce and butter. Season to taste with salt and pepper. Serve immediately.

Index

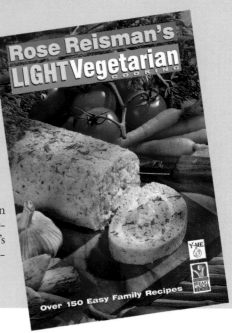

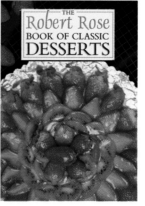

ROBERT ROSE

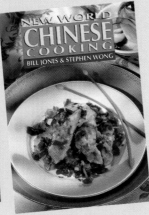

In *New World Noodles,* Bill Jones and Stephen Wong have created the next step in pasta books. Here's a fresh approach to mealtime, blending Eastern and Western flavors to give you a wide range of tantalizing dishes.

ISBN 1-896503-01-2

Take the best of Chinese cooking and put it together with an imaginative variety of North American ingredients. What have you got? The next step in Chinese cookbooks — *New World Chinese Cooking.* Easy, accessible and delicious!

ISBN 1-896503-70-5

Here's Mediterranean cooking at its best. Taste all the wonderfully fresh flavors of this sun-filled region, with over 100 dishes from Italy, France, Greece, Spain, Turkey and North Africa. They're as delicious as they are easy to prepare.

ISBN 1-896503-68-3

Byron Ayanoglu's *The New Vegetarian Gourmet* creates fast and easy culinary magic. These exquisite vegetarian recipes are a must for people who love great-tasting food but want all the benefits of vegetarian meals.

ISBN 1-896503-26-8

Johanna Burkhard's *Comfort Food Cookbook* brings you over 100 fast, easy recipes for the most comforting dishes you've ever tasted, fully updated for today's families. So relax. This is the kind of old-fashioned food that just makes you feel good.

ISBN 1-896503-07-1

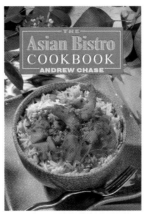

With *The Asian Bistro Cookbook,* Andrew Chase brings you all the best of China, Japan and Thailand — plus tantalizing dishes from the Philippines and Korea, as well as Vietnam, Indonesia and Taiwan. They're unusual and they're delicious.

ISBN 1-896503-21-7

AVAILABLE AT BOOKSTORES AND OTHER FINE RETAILERS

More of your favorite recipes

Just about everyone loves pasta. After all, there are few types of food that can be prepared in so many interesting ways. And that's what you'll discover in this book — over 50 recipes that range from classic comfort foods such as macaroni and cheese to more exotic Asian-inspired noodle dishes.   ISBN 1-896503-74-8

Here's a book for all the people who love desserts, but worry about the fat and calories. Imagine being able to indulge, guilt-free, in luscious cheesecakes, pies — even chocolate desserts! Well, now you can. Choose from a variety of after-dinner treats that contain less than 200 calories per serving.   ISBN 1-896503-72-1

Want something quick, easy and delicious? Then here's the book for you. Whether it's snacks for your kids, a light salad for lunch, or appetizers for dinner-party guests, you'll find just the right thing in this collection of 50 great recipes. They're winners every time.
ISBN 1-896503-51-9

Cook along with bestselling author Rose Reisman as she prepares over 50 of her favorite dishes — including soups, burgers, chili and cheesecakes. Each section features helpful, step-by-step pictures that demonstrate a particular technique. Over 100 color images in all.
ISBN 1-896503-28-4